Volatile Texts: Us Two

Zsuzsanna Gahse

VOLATILE TEXTS: US TWO

Translated from the German by Chenxin Jiang

DALKEY ARCHIVE PRESS

Originally published in German as
Instabile Texte by Edition Korrespondenzen in 2005.

Copyright © 2005 by Zsuzsanna Gahse
Translation copyright © 2016 by Chenxin Jiang
First Dalkey Archive edition, 2017.

Library of Congress Cataloging-in-Publication Data
Names: Gahse, Zsuzsanna, 1946- author. | Jiang, Chenxin, translator.
Title: Volatile texts : us two / Zsuzzanna Gahse ; translated by Chenxin Jiang.
Other titles: Instabile texte. English
Description: 1st dalkey archive ed. | Victoria, TX : Dalkey Archive Press,
2016. | "Originally published in German as Instabile Texte by Edition
Korrespondenzen [Wien] in 2005" -- Verso title page.
Identifiers: LCCN 2016010728 | ISBN 9781628971361 (pbk. : alk. paper)
Subjects: LCSH: Language and languages--Fiction. |
Multilingualism--Fiction.
| Europe--Fiction. | Switzerland--Fiction. | GSAFD: Love stories.
Classification: LCC PT2667.A34 I6713 2016 | DDC 833/.92--dc23
LC record available at https://lccn.loc.gov/2016010728

swiss arts council

pr☉helvetia

Partially funded by a grant by the Illinois Arts Council, a state agency.
Published in collaboration with the Swiss Arts Council Pro Helvetia, Zurich.

www.dalkeyarchive.com
Victoria, TX / McLean, IL / Dublin

Dalkey Archive Press publications are, in part, made possible through the
support of the University of Houston-Victoria and its programs in creative
writing, publishing, and translation.

Translator's Preface

Zsuzsanna Gahse's Switzerland is a place where every valley has its own language and "every person is translated"—a perfect microcosm of Europe, the continent that consists of a mélange of accents, languages, and landscapes. Over thirteen short chapters that wander through the Swiss Alps, Gahse asks the question: what does the difficulty of being European have to do with the difficulty of being in love?

Volatile Texts centers on what the narrator identifies as the quintessentially European act of geographical and linguistic wandering. Gahse's own biography is relevant to both themes; she was born in 1946 in Budapest and grew up in Vienna and Kassel after her parents fled Hungary during the 1956 uprising. Shortly after *Volatile Texts* was published, she was awarded the Robert Bosch Foundation's prestigious Adelbert von Chamisso Prize for authors whose native language is not German; *Volatile Texts* is set in her current place of residence, Switzerland. When Gahse learned of the Chamisso Prize she resisted being labeled as an emigrant, much as she affirms that speaking a non-Indo-European language (Hungarian) has been enriching.* Like Gahse

* Email from the author, 26 March 2016.

herself, the narrator finds an affinity for "Beckett, Oscar Wilde, Gertrude Stein, Gombrowicz, Ödön von Horváth, and others, writers who didn't live in their country or even necessarily for their country, I decided that this was precisely what made them good writers." She too considers herself a migrant for whom settling down somewhere is only one stage of an ongoing journey, and the rhythm of Gahse's long sentences mirrors the meandering quality of the narrator's travels.

Just as German words like *Tulpe* (tulip) and *Rose* (rose) can have foreign origins even if they don't sound foreign at all ("Don't Say Anything"), migrants can gradually take on qualities of the landscape they live in, and some of the book's most compelling passages convey Gahse's affection for her adopted Alpine home. "No one is independent of his surroundings," she writes. "If someone looks into the distance, he'll feel distant; if he looks at bright light, he'll feel bright; if he looks at fog, he'll feel foggy." Migrating to or inhabiting a place is significant because of how people are shaped by their environments. While the questions of what migration entails for Europe and what being European means have only grown larger in the public imagination since *Volatile Texts* was first published, Europe/Europa, the mythical Phoenician princess and narrator of the first chapter, would point out that such questions are as old as Europe itself.

Volatile Texts begins with a piece called "A Collection," a title that draws attention to the organizational principle that governs the narrator's Alpine wandering. The "volatile" texts are a collection of thirteen pieces whose lack of clear hierarchy or narrative destination belies their underlying continuities. The effect created by assembling such a collection resembles that of the technique of *découpé*. In her Chamisso Prize lecture, Gahse explains that she once kept a record of the changes in the light as it played on the lake by her house. She then cut up the text and rearranged it to form the chapter "Logbook of Light." The sense of fluctuating color and fleeting impressions created by these aleatory juxtapositions is ideally suited to a study of light on a single lake, but also to *Volatile Texts* as a collection of interconnected stories set in a single location, Switzerland. Gahse reports that "the reshuffled texts (almost of their own accord) revealed new coherences"; the Europe she depicts is just such a reshuffled continent.* In these short pieces, she narrows down the continental scale of new linguistic and migratory coherences to a ride in a small plane, a man whose head turns into a lightbulb, and an eerie woman called Berta who tells tall tales.

The protagonist of this collection of stories is the individual word, its history and affinities. The German word for eye, for instance, is described as being "very old, a beautiful word," one that has retained its original sense, remaining "as it is, without breaking, which is why it's with your *Augen* that you see." *Volatile Texts* delights in words and the resonances between them. In translation, I have sought wherever possible to find parallels for these puns in English. For example, in the sentence:

* "Das Vergnügen an dieser Operation war, dass die neu gemischten Texte beinahe von selbst neue Zusammenhänge zeigten." Interview with Antje Weber: "Straßen der Sprache. Die Schriftstellerin Zsuzsanna Gahse erhält den Adelbert-von-Chamisso-Preis," *Süddeutsche Zeitung*, 15 February 2006.

> We keep going, we're going on, to drive you have to be
> driven, motivated, going forward, words like conduct-
> ing and directing are all related to the act of driving, all
> related to the question of *for,*

I use for/forward, driving/driven to render the wordplay in
Gahse's use of *Für/führen/fürstlich/fahren.* Elsewhere, when
Gahse notices that *schmeißen, rühren,* and *schmettern* all
have etymological roots related to the word *werfen* (throw),
her observation calls for three English words with a common etymological root: my translation incorporates the
words *warp, reject,* and *hyperbole,* which all have etymological shadows of the meaning "to throw."

Gahse's attention to how linguistic, auditory, and physical environments shape a person's inner life motivates her
interest in what might be called the phenomenology of
modern life. "Anyhowever" is an idiosyncratic account of
the dreaded earworm, the impossibility of getting rid of a
tune that has lodged itself firmly in one's head, in which the
hapless narrator finds her mental space suddenly invaded by
"constant musical programming" consisting of her entire
vocabulary of popular music. "Seeing and Hearing" reflects
instead on how the flattening effect of the bird's-eye view
from a plane shapes the traveler's perception of landscape.
Finally, every single paragraph in the book's final chapter is
precisely "320 Characters" long, a constraint I replicate in
the translation. This dates *Volatile Texts* to pre-smartphone
days; 320 is the maximum number of characters in a two-
part GSM message. The individual pieces in this volatile

collection translate a litany of worries about unemployment into a Muzak-like, multilingual stream of pop songs, a mountainous landscape into an aerial view, a romantic entanglement into a series of text messages.

* * *

Whereas the notion of "volatile" suggests that the text is contingent, unfinished, the product of migratory instability, the subtitle "us two" hints at the book's invisible protagonist, the narrator's travel companion. Gradually it emerges that the travels during which the narrator rediscovers Switzerland are secret trysts with her lover, Pierre. Together, they explore the city of Lausanne, taking the subway down to the lakefront, chatting to strangers in restaurants, and being interrogated by the police after a woman is murdered in their hotel.

But this is not the only or even necessarily the primary love story in the book. For Gahse, "Europe is a collection of languages as well as wrinkles, and love is part of every collection." The provisional bonds that hold a collection together are analogous to the unstable bonds of love. In this sense, "Europe is a love story too." Yet it turns out that the story she has in mind is the rape of Europa by Zeus—a deeply ambivalent "love story," at best. The difficulty of both being in love and of living in or traveling through Europe is figured throughout *Volatile Texts* as the problem of translation. The narrator enthuses that "the fact that so much is translated is one of the most wonderful of European accomplishments." But then she adds, somewhat ruefully:

"Translation so often leads to misunderstanding." And elsewhere: "Unfortunately, the original would have been the ideal, who wouldn't rather have the original, the non-translation is what people want."

In the final two chapters, as Pierre and the narrator cope with the gradient of urban Lausanne, they are continually translating the past and future tenses of their relationship into the "steep grammar" of the city, the literary affairs of Russian novels into their Swiss present. Just as it is impossible for lovers to understand each other's "contrary, contradictory, incompatible, meaningless, unrealistic" expectations without discussing them, it is impossible for two Europeans—perhaps even two speakers of Swiss German from different villages—to understand each other without translation. The volatility of both being in love and being European derives from the fact that two people cannot understand each other without some form of mediation; the necessity of translation only makes that need for mediation explicit.

Chenxin Jiang

Volatile Texts: Us Two

1

A Collection

THE ALPS FORM A CRESCENT that stretches across Europe like a croissant-shaped *Kipferl*. Within these mountains lies Switzerland, shaped like a round bun, and Switzerland is Europe. Switzerland is disintegrating into its valleys—there is such loneliness on the mountaintops! (*Kipferl* isn't a word that all people know; nor is *Gipfeli*, the Swiss-German word for a croissant; there isn't anything that people all over Europe know.)

Europe is disintegrating, the old lady is falling apart. She recently appeared at the Museum Festival with a terrible heap of jewelry around her neck; she'd just dyed her hair blond; above her fake gold necklace hung her wretched, worn face, and then she laughed, walked up to the bar, embraced a tall young man, and drew him up to her lips to kiss him artfully.

Europe consists of its disintegration. Europe is disintegrating into its individual valleys. The valleys are boundaries dividing one mountain from the next, each mountain from the others. And the old lady looks frightful.

Europe has high, high peaks with valleys between them,

and the mothers drive their children into the ravines, up to the cliffs. They say that a different people lives in each valley; a few years ago they had only four languages between them, but since then they've further divided the languages, each valley has a language, there's still only one language per valley, but soon there will be many more, as time passes and everything matures. All kinds of accents and even all kinds of words lie in the wrinkles, the valleys, if Switzerland is Europe. Eventually (this word is common to all the valleys), every person will be recognizable by her language, by the attitude of her mouth. Even to the north and west of this country, the timbre of a voice can function as a geographical clue, as in the warring southeast, where people create distance between themselves via accents; creating distance via dialects happens here too, all kinds of sounds set the tone in mountains, caves, and lakes.

A collection of wrinkles, mountain ridges wrinkling the earth.

But now that all the roads are being rebuilt constantly, the roads themselves are carving a constant course toward a great continental future. Office buildings gape emptily from the curb, peering down at the streets until the streets are razed and moved elsewhere and everything that was in them has been swiftly rearranged; streets coursing all the way to the borders and up into the mountains as well, into a future with new streets that lead into all the valleys, the valleys in which these most diverse languages are spoken.

No one can learn more than two or three of these languages, and people only retain things they can actually grasp, but the accents are gliding further and further apart, especially the vowels, as though the vowels weren't open sounds but private ones, so that there's barely a single word that everyone in Europe knows. Of course everyone keeps trying to learn as many words as possible, but that isn't easy when people barely understand and often misunderstand each other.

A collection of languages. Words drop out, fall out of use, and when they do, you may never again be able to say the things those words meant.

Collecting junk is part of collecting languages, all kinds of junk; of course there are no figures for how many pairs of pantyhose are torn in Europe each day, and the past and future of interesting and uninteresting items of clothing remain obscure, although these things should have a say, and not only because they create so much junk.

Sunset. It is evening.

At the Museum Festival not too long ago she said she wanted to be overwhelmed. She was soon overwhelmed, because portraits of her were hanging on all the walls, even if these portraits of her as a young woman represented nothing more than the artists' imaginations. Nonetheless, there is something unmistakable about Europa, about the sudden eruption of her expansive gestures. No matter how old she is, she still tries to surprise with her eruptions.

She is bruised, formed like lava, old, ugly, yet still alluring, an extremely opaque lady, not really a lady, but a woman. Little is known about her emotional life, and she remains adamantly silent on that point.

To put it in more technical terms:

He (whoever he is) was born in Hamburg and then lived

in Munich; he was born in Hamburg, spent two years in Paris, and then moved to Rome, a Hamburger. He was born into the world in Hamburg, but he lived in Kiev, and then later in Mělník, which made him Czech; he lived there for a while—the Hamburger was a Czech—and some years later he went to Rome. There, one evening, he met the man who had been born in Zurich and lived in Geneva; the Genoan arrived, and it was a significant evening for both Romans. They arranged to meet again in Graz, and the wife of one of the two Romans also came along; she was not Roman and had never been to either Rome or Hamburg, but was born in Baar and grew up in Ticino, and now she was driving with the two Romans to Graz, which made them all Austrians. It goes without saying that someone from Hamburg has had quite different experiences than someone from Switzerland—where you belong isn't a matter of indifference—but they decided to travel to Italy together, and at the border they met an American woman who noticed the extra spot in their car and wanted to join them. Now there was an American sitting next to the Austrians. Having spent three weeks in America, she was busy readjusting; she kept referring to *jet lag* in English, but the Austrians couldn't understand the American because she had a French accent. You can get used to an accent, of course. They arrived in Genoa, those Genoans.

As he was speaking, three women from newspapers and two from magazines stood next to him, taking notes and waiting for the interview that would follow, while the artists' wives were also waiting and pinning up their hair, and then the photographers came. But things hadn't gone that far yet, it was a very long process. It must be said that his speech made his listeners feel at home: the gallery owners were nodding, the women from the newspapers and magazines took more notes, and the artists listened. The artists had arrived almost on time, so they had been able to catch the beginning of the speech, and even their wives, insofar as they had come with their wives, were listening—it's a woman's job to listen—and the women from newspapers and magazines naturally took notes so as to later ask relevant questions in their interviews with the artists; the talented gallery owners were silent, and the speaker spoke in such a way that even the artists listened, as well as their wives, insofar as they had come with their wives; the art historian was there, as well as the gallery owners, remaining silent about their own talents, while the women from the newspapers and magazines took some notes, and that's when the photographers came, while the artists listened cautiously, their faces turned toward the speaker, who was slowly arriving at the end of his speech, and their wives, insofar as they had come with their wives, were laughing—it's a woman's job to laugh—pinning up their hair, when the photographers arrived, and as the master of the room slowly got to the end of his speech, it struck him that one of the artists' wives was pretty to look at, and all that while the women from the newspaper were cautiously noting down what he said, waiting for the interview to begin, while the artists, standing next to the gallery owners, bowed their heads, so that the gallery owners looked at the wives . . .

Next to the door stood a man who had nothing to do with this crowd and didn't feel at home among them; he looked as though he would rather be elsewhere; he was easy to overlook, which is to say that he didn't blend in, he blended out, a man with a southern face, probably a Roman.

She lay on a slate slab, propping herself up with one elbow, and for some reason she put up her hair with her other hand, the woman from Hamburg. In the meantime she looked into the milky sun, barely aware of her own feelings. Three men, artists, were hard at work doing portraits of her.

Of course Europe is a collection of languages as well as wrinkles, and love is part of every collection. In this sense Europe is a love story too.

Despite her age, and despite the fact that no one wants to look into her bitter face, she's never considered backing down. Her rightful place is where she's standing, as she pointed out recently at a demonstration where many women gathered.

It isn't true that Europeans don't want to be loved; Europeans want love, and when this desire isn't fulfilled, war breaks out. This desire is never fulfilled.

Whenever Europeans are bitterly unloved, they go shopping, and then they can see: that's where love has gone. In Spain at least there are bullfights, people ask themselves where the bull comes from and look at him, and that's interesting; it's very European (which is to say: very much Europa), you can hardly imagine Europa or Europe without bulls.

But the story of the bull goes way back. Although much has changed since then, many women still have a bit of

Europa in them (which means they're either afraid of bulls or love them, Hemingway has already said everything else there is to say about these powerful animals).

In this wrinkled collection of a continent certain words remain unintelligible. If those words are translated anyway—and it's one of the most wonderful of European accomplishments that they so often are—the view becomes clearer, and now you can see a huge, green, mossy, steep field, beneath which there are streets running through the mountains, and cows and bulls grazing separately on the fields. Cows, bulls, mossy fields. As it flies over the landscape from east to west, trailing a dark shadow far beneath it, the plane makes the landscape smaller.

The fact that so much is translated is one of the most wonderful European accomplishments, even though translation so often leads to misunderstanding.

Not long before the outbreak of the war in Yugoslavia, a young Slovene found a package somewhere near Sarajevo. In an attic. It contained several notebooks and loose bits of paper, probably Europa's latest notes and diaries. They were fragmentary, unpublished private jottings. Here follows an excerpt from this material:

I very much doubt that European languages will simply drift apart. Quite the contrary. When else have there been so many words that mean the same thing in every country, even if they don't mean much on their own? Everyone understands the words *stop*, *go*, and *okay*, as well as so many other signs, signals, symbols, icons. I only wonder how it'll ever be possible to talk about these symbols. Right now this is the most pressing question I have.

It makes no sense to appear as a bull when people are expecting a swan, but he had to attempt to appear as a bull.

And it wasn't honest of him to be passing himself off as a bull, he made a dishonest start, since he was only imitating the sort of bull that remains a bull under all circumstances. Being a real bull, which he certainly wanted to be, would have been more honest.

According to my name I'm a European and I have no intention of backing down. On the contrary, I want to name everything after me. In the beginning only a tiny stretch of eastern Europe had my name, but the term spread westward, into the sunset, until my name stretched from the Urals to the ocean. That wasn't how it was in the beginning: the somewhat hidden root of my name is actually *Erev*, meaning sunset, the evening laying itself down upon the earth, the sun setting toward darkness. Erev, calls the young man at the bar; I'll never let him go; I know what I'm entitled to, and he knows all too well that the darkness and sunset he's been dreaming of won't stop at the ocean, it'll cross over to the next continent, where they also speak my languages; America has long belonged to me, and I will proceed further westward, across the next ocean, westward to Asia, where I've already arrived, till I end up where I'm from. (Or rather, something that started with me will end up there, but I don't claim to know precisely what.)

And I think there's also a technical way of describing this: My name is Erev, and my memory remains good as I keep going, full of wrinkles and folds, all the way back to Asia. The young men will keep that in mind, talented as they are, while the young women will turn resolutely away in disgust, but they too will grow old and so grow either subdued or talented. The women from the newspapers and magazines stand on one side with the first wrinkles, and the men stand on the other side. And over there, on the other continent, they speak my language, and during my speech, which is still about the powerful or about power or sometimes also about bulls, the gallery owners are pinning their hair up, and the artists and their wives, or at least the ones that came with their wives, are listening attentively. I go on speaking, my speech is currently about Geneva—I am Genovese—I'm speaking calmly to artists and women on the subject of rubble, collecting rubble in Switzerland, on the dialectical disintegration of languages and of other collections, I'm pinning my hair up and waving with both hands at the young man over there, while here, in this place, it grows dark, night has come.

I have to get a facelift. It's not that I used to be much better looking when I was younger. Ancient crones are hideous, I know, at least some of them are, but gradually, gradually, they can begin to look less ugly.

A thought looks like a knot. Just like *Kipferls* or buns, thoughts have a certain correct form, a real form that has neither beginning nor end and is visible from every angle. And the form of a thought, although thoughts all look different, doesn't really have a beginning, thoughts run their course, they run in different directions, even if they will always be knots, and besides, even Europe has an external form without beginning or end, as Europe runs westward toward Asia.

I feel at home in Asia. I just took a look in the mirror, I don't like that young man anymore, and I absolutely must collect myself.

2

Logbook of Light

THE LAKE LEAPS AQUAMARINE out of its basin. What's happened to it this bright morning!

This particular light belongs to this particular day. It also belongs to this place, and elsewhere the same light would look altogether different; but the place doesn't belong to me. To whom can a place belong, I wonder, as I look at it.

Mt. Rigi. Mt. Rigi. Mt. Rigi disappears in the fog, she appears again, and disappears in the fog. That's how the day passes. (In the meantime I have learned that although the word *Berg* or mountain is masculine in German, a particular *Berg*, like Mt. Rigi, can be feminine. Mt. Rigi is feminine, both when she's wrapped in fog and when she's naked.) These recordings are mine; I hold exclusive rights to them.

I have to limit the number of positions from which I view the mountain, otherwise my freedom will disintegrate into randomness. Randomness, light, water, freedom, mountains, freedom, lake, dark, bright, medium-gray, cheerful, medium-gray freedom, bright cheerful lake, dark light, randomness, water.

It's 3 in the afternoon and the photon war has begun,

bullets fly into the lake and shoot out sideways and straight up from it while passersby rub their eyes, there are tears of light in their eyes.

The light has a headache.

Yesterday: light

Today: light

Tomorrow: light.

Highway-fog, mountain-railway-fog, mountain-fog, lake-fog, bright forest-fog, green forest-fog in the spring, stream-gray, stone-gray, head-gray, mental-gray with coffee, with a cup of stale coffee cooling on the desk, sitting-at-desk-fog, silhouette-fog, blinking red chimney-fog-light, street-fog, night-fog, daytime-room-darkness in the fog, fog-laughter, fog-indifference, reading a newspaper in the fog.

Certain words are mountains here, especially prepositions, many of them, until all the jagged and beveled and rounded edges and all the *in front ofs* and *behinds* can be seen from every angle. We're talking about mountain spaces, about the details of being *behind* and *through* and *in front of.* From between Mt. Rigi and Mt. Ross, behind them, the sun shines on two sloped monsters. Maybe they are what people call myths.

Nonetheless, in the past nine days there have been twelve deaths in the mountains, one and a half deaths per day. For the past week, the lake has had goose pimples every day in the late afternoon, and it is so terrified that it shivers all day long.

As a result of the recession, there have been no colors

for the past six weeks. But no one's been saving any money, people have simply lost interest in buying things, because even the shelves are stocked with gray goods.

Ladies and Gentlemen, as you know, we have been enveloped in fog for days, and I have taken it upon myself to write about the question of relating to light. The very question of light and of relating to it is relevant wherever you are, and yet it seems to have nothing to do with real, compelling, ongoing life, which makes the subject of my talk sound uncertain and unstable. The fog and the fact that it's been impossible to see anything make it even harder to talk about light, especially now that it's May. I must admit that day-fog is very different from night-fog here. The difference was especially clear today. We were sitting in the tavern called The Pigeon, it was in the late afternoon and hence it was light out, and I could have sworn we were in a tavern somewhere in the mountains, up on a peak with a cliff falling just beyond the window, because we sat there drinking good wine, and there was nothing outside. Nothing gaped outside, and it grew dark. Then a ship sailed by, a vessel hung with strings of glowing lights which couldn't have been in the mountains, and we fell away from our mountain illusion and came back to the lake.

Someone said we would be shoveled full of light, all eyes shining, showing skin on a summer evening; and the walls of the houses, the marquees, the tables, the glasses, and the artificial cacti all slaked their thirst on the huge, flat, red-orange evening that is rising from the lake.

At night the lake is a black hole and the edges of the hole

are lit up as far as the eye can see. The question of how far the eye can see presents itself at every opportunity involving light. Eye-light.

Yesterday: light

Today: light

Tomorrow: light.

Yesterday: light; today: light; tomorrow: light. Light has a clear affiliation: it belongs to the day.

There's no great difference between weather and light. Though it must be said that "great" is just as vague a word as "beautiful," and words can be very vague.

Everyone loves particular characteristics *out of* other people. Precisely: out of them. Each person loves something particular out of another person. A particular brightness. To be able to love the south face out of Mt. Rigi, that would be something.

The weather is forecast separately for each mountain and valley here, there are splinter forecasts, personal weather outcomes for the tiniest stretches of land. It's enough to drive you crazy. The general sense of disquiet in these mountains and lakes is enough to drive you crazy. In the mountains, on the lakes, in the mountains, on the lakes, in the mountains, on the lakes, the light in the mountains on the lakes is enough to drive you crazy, the surplus, it could drive you crazy, I have to hold still. Sometimes that's just what it's like.

That's just what it's like sometimes.

The light breaks into pieces, it's beside itself.

In any case, each time of day is unmistakably connected to its respective brightness; between 3 p.m. and 3:50 everything looks silver. That's just what it's like: silver clouds, silver lake, silver light, dull, unpolished silver. Light and time reminds you of space and time, and light is certainly not independent of space. The silver has disappeared, the mountains have disappeared, Mt. Pilatus and Mt. Rigi can no longer be seen, there is nothing but fog.

The light has a headache.

Highway-fog, mountain-railway-fog, lake-fog, bright forest-fog, green forest-fog in the spring, stream-gray, head-gray, morning-gray with a cup of coffee in the darkness of the kitchen.

Of course there is light and darkness, which is simply day and night. I should have realized that immediately.

We'll leave this sky to the gulls and the pigeons!

All night long, light tumbles and turns in the firm belief that physical exercise holds the soul together, and being a healthy soul, it imagines its way through the night, it's a thoroughly healthy light, its body only stays so fresh because of its bright thoughts, which allow it to keep doing inner gymnastics. Light is the great Turner. (William Turner.)

Light has a clear affiliation, it belongs to the day. These recordings are mine; I hold exclusive rights to them.

Today the rough metal sea reflects a somewhat smooth blue-white sky. Today lake-light predominates, and perhaps it will reach all the way to the sky. Maybe one day the lake will be so bright that it is made of glass, and then I will be able to look all the way through it. Ladies and Gentlemen, we'll leave this sky to the gulls and the pigeons!

The lake leaps aquamarine out of its basin. What's happened to it this bright morning! At 9:00 a.m. it sinks whitely back into the basin and reflects the banks. At 11:00 it is a lake like other lakes, the rippling water is concerned with itself and pays no attention to the sky and banks. By evening it has turned inward, retreated into itself, and its far western edge is clearly white.

I should have realized that immediately.

This is a logbook.

Some dictionaries record that the word "light" can denote an inward impression, that light can be an idea. That I can easily see. An idea shines over the lake again, and even in the lofty Alps it's made an impression. Lake Zug thinks bright white, it usually thinks alone and refrains from taking an interest in people. It is a lonely lake that serves a strange purpose for many strangers and has grown accustomed to looking away.

During the moments in which the lake loses its mirror, there is no light in either the mountains or the skies. At that point its surroundings begin to wait nervously. Only at times like that, but never all day long, the lake is beside itself. It has never rained all day. *It rained all day* is a sentence, and nothing more. It has also never been dark for an entire day. And it's also not true that there are no more shadows. Nothing is always true. Nothing is always. Today I looked under the cars on the street, searching for their shadows, and it was hard to find shapes that corresponded to cars, but I could tell that no day is completely shadowless.

Enter the tragic. Finally, the dark sky in the west fell heavily into the lake, to the east the sky was white with terror, the clock tower cowered, Mt. Pilatus was missing, as it often is, and I ran from window to window.

There is no great difference between weather and light.

Though it must be said that "great" is just as vague a word as "beautiful"—interestingly, words can be very vague. Today the weather sank in the form of a haze onto the hills to the west, a good day for chores, a washday hangs over the lake, today work will get done, and because of that the weather offers little color, there is a workday sunniness about it that is not dreary. A nice workday, and the light, too, is nice but not colorful. On Swiss radio weather reports, a warm and colorful day is announced as a "beautiful day." In Germany the same kind of weather is announced on weather reports as a "fine day." You could simply call it good weather. Beautiful, fine, and good all mean the same thing.

The lake leaps aquamarine out of its basin. What's happened to it this bright morning!

Later that evening all eyes will be shining as if something might happen that very moment, and the walls of the houses, the marquees, the tables, and the glasses will all have slaked their thirst on the huge, flat, red-orange evening that is rising from the lake.

It is almost 7 in the evening, and I know that the people who are walking west along the street and on the banks of the lake will have a striking love-light in their faces until long past 9.

The water is pink-orange. Beautiful. Pink-orange is a beautiful color. The lake reflects the late evening sun, and it's beautiful. Anyway, evenings in Zug are always beautiful as long as the weather is reasonably good. Blood-red, no news. As long as there's no news or other unpleasant events, blood-red is a beautiful color.

Something turquoise was glowing on the neighbor's

porch, and it turned out to be some panties entangled in a pair of black pantyhose. Panties and pantyhose lay twisted together on the floor, what would I think of this evident haste if I were a man, in fact, what am I thinking right now. The last night of May is over, and I am looking forward to June.

Anyway, I know each individual needs a certain amount of excitement.

There's a flash of summer thunder outside, and of course, on the opposite bank, the storm alert system is blinking.

The birds are back in the sky.

The rear half of the lake is glowing like a powerful lamp. Mt. Pilatus has appeared again.

The whole lake is a lamp, I can't look at it, the lake-lamp will blind me.

Nonetheless, in the past nine days there have been twelve deaths in the mountains, one and a half deaths per day.

The birds are sitting in a line, marking the boundary between the city and the lake, and the water is pink-orange. Pink-orange is beautiful. The lake reflects the late evening sun. Anyway, evenings in Zug are always beautiful as long as the weather is decent. As long as there's no news or other unpleasant events, blood-red is beautiful. The birds are not yet asleep. Back at my desk, light plays across the sky. We'll leave this sky to the gulls and the pigeons. Luckily there's also a plane crossing the sky. Isn't it something to see a plane!

It's enough to drive you crazy. It's enough to drive you crazy, the general sense of disquiet in these mountains and lakes, the light is enough to drive you crazy, the surplus, I have to hold still.

Extended bouts of light-constipation can give you big ugly pores, and once it starts, it only gets worse, like anything that is allowed to really begin. For instance, when an end has begun, it can only go on ending. When an ending begins, it goes on until it ends. And when something begins, it goes on until the beginning has come to an end.

The lake lies calm and off to one side. Not melancholy but empty. My soul has gone so far that it has emptied the landscape.

A great death is closing in, it's coming nearer, it's a particular death, whose death is it. I know that two of the deaths belonged to nightfall, they were suicides, self-darkenings. One man shot himself because his group didn't need him anymore, and the other threw himself off a building.

Yesterday: light, today: light. But even when the act of observing extends across the lake and is linked to particular dates and times, it is timeless. Outside of world and time. Whatever happens now, I already know that each individual needs a certain amount of excitement, regardless of what is happening to him and how trivial it is. Each person gets from his circumstances the level of shock that he needs at any given point in time.

A few years ago, the question was how you would want to die if you had to die a violent death. Many women said at the time that they would like to be eaten by a crocodile. They must all have had a certain mental picture of a crocodile, perhaps of how cold crocodiles are. Maybe a crocodile isn't cold on the inside at all, and out there you can't tell how cold the water is, but at the time they gave an answer that would now be considered cool.

The fishermen say that they go out onto the lake at night, and I too am no longer going back to daylight, I don't want to look out and wait until I see something.

Later I would dream of a stormy sea-like lake. The water kept rising, it raged, it was beside itself, it shot up into the air so that there was nothing but water. Then someone explained to me that no matter how high the water levels were, the water would only cover part of the mountains, and the mountains would still be higher.

In the lake I see a man. I am against seeing this lake-man, against the gendered German nouns that cause men to appear in the sea, in the mountains, the lakebed becomes a man, every tree on the banks becomes a man, as does every fish. What should I be looking for out on the lake when I'm surrounded by these men, none of whom is a real man, all of whom are cartoon men who only remind me of possible men; they remind you of men, they used to remind you of men at a point when you thought you had figured out what a man and a woman are, and that's what some people believe even today; even today, a man-fish, a man-tree, a man-mountain and a lake-man. A man-lake, I mean. I am, at the moment, the only woman among all these non-men, and there isn't a single real person around me. Or rather, there is someone else here: the night! I am not the woman here; she is, she and her men. *Die Nacht* is feminine. I love her, but she is masculine to me. Even the night is a man to me, I have to admit it!

Finally, an opinion-bright morning.

The Alps are starting now, and they can stop whenever they want to. The Alps are stopping. The people change ever so slightly, they become cooler or hotter, and the Alps change too.

Tomorrow the clouds everywhere will revolt, to show that it is they who organize the day-light and night-light, tomorrow all the clouds will disappear, and the sky will be so blue that even the sun will be blue. The blue will shine.

Finally, an opinion-bright morning.

Yesterday: light, today: light, tomorrow: light.

Maybe one day the lake will become so bright that it will be made of glass. Even though there have been twelve deaths in the mountains in the last nine days. That's just what it's like sometimes.

Now I love the light less, it hardly matters to me anymore. How one's interest fades! Suddenly there it is again, faintly. It's actually anger, a palpable anger, but in the afternoon the background has changed, the requirements have changed. Now I like the lake again, especially at night.

Someone said we would be shoveled full of light, all eyes shining, everyone has skin on summer evenings, and the walls of the houses, the marquees, the tables, the glasses, the artificial cacti would slake their thirst on the huge, flat, red-orange evening that was rising from the lake.

At night the lake is a black hole and the edges of the hole are lit up. As far as the eye can see.

These recordings are mine; I hold exclusive rights to them.

Light has a clear affiliation, it belongs to the day. It twirls and turns, it's a great turner. The great Turner!

On the other hand, I am certain that no one is independent of his surroundings. If someone looks into the distance, he'll feel distant, if he looks into bright light, he'll feel bright, if he looks at narrow, high mountains, he'll feel narrow, if he looks at high, distant mountains, he'll feel high and distant.

Everyone loves particular characteristics *out of* other people. I really mean: out of them. Everyone loves something particular out of someone else.

If I live to be a hundred, I will have spent one percent of my life in Zug. But if I should only live to be fifty, it will have been two percent. Two percent is the return I'm presently earning on my German savings account.

And then there is the view, by day and night, the Alps will start before long, and they can stop whenever they like. The Alps break off and end.

The fishermen fish at night.

Maybe one day the lake will become so bright it's made of glass, and then I'll be able to look all the way through it. That future light would also be intriguing. This evening, for instance, I'm going up to Mt. Zugerberg and can already make a prediction that is neither professional nor objective. I already know that the sky up on Mt. Zugerberg will be bigger than it is down in the city. And tomorrow the clouds everywhere will revolt, to show that it is they who organize the day-light and night-light, tomorrow all the clouds will disappear, and the sky will be so blue that even the sun will be blue. The blue will shine.

Now I love it less, it hardly matters to me anymore. How one's interest fades! Suddenly there it is again, faintly.

Some time ago my sunglasses slipped from my hand and

fell into the water, and their black lenses were visible for a long time as they continued to sink, and when I called for help, a man came right away and fished a pair of sunglasses from the lakebed for me, but they weren't mine.

In the meantime, it has become a known fact that not just the inhabitants of Zug, but anyone who lives by a lake, dreams more frequently of water than do other people. The environment you experience by day won't let you off easily at night, and it is the case that dreams of water are related to having a blue soul, which means that people around lakes have more soul than other people do, or at the very least, that they spend more time with their inner blue than other people do, and that difference is telling.

Later I would dream of a stormy sea-like lake. The water kept rising, it raged, it was beside itself, it shot up into the air so that there was nothing but water. Then someone explained to me that no matter how high the water levels were, the water would only cover part of the mountains, and the mountains would still be higher.

But I am against seeing a man in the lake, one in every single mountain too, every tree on the banks is a man, to say nothing of all those fish, and everyone around me is supposed to always have known what to expect of a masculine noun and what it looks like. I have to learn by heart that a fish is masculine, except that fish-women, mermaids, exist too; just learn the genders by heart and you'll be fine, they tell me, or was what they once told me, and that's what they believe today, even today; and out on the lake, in the middle of the night, I am supposed to imagine that the night—of all things, the night—is feminine, which isn't easy to do at night.

The light comes from the water, from the reflection in the water and probably depends on how deep the water is. Depth is feminine, she's my friend. I have a female girlfriend. Otherwise I have few female friends, something I regret, sometimes I'm glad that's the case, most of the time I regret it. Most of the time I feel as though my female friends haven't yet emerged from the depths or disappeared into them.

I can still see the medium-high mountain range in the west, irrespective of my concerns it stands where it stands, it's sometimes green and sometimes brown, sometimes partway between green and brown, sometimes enveloped in fog, and I, the observer, am overwhelmed by the daily production, but I cannot see the medium-high mountain range on the other side of the lake, it's impressive how it remains so separate, so indifferent to my mood, I would like to describe it separate from my mood, and it's really interesting that it can stay that way, that day after day the mountain and light remain independent of the people, just like the lake, while I myself am certain that people are not independent of their surroundings. If someone looks into the distance, he'll feel distant; if he looks at bright light, he'll feel bright; if he looks at high, narrow mountains, he'll feel narrow; if he looks at high, distant mountains, he'll feel high and distant; if he looks at medium-high mountains, he'll feel middling; if he looks into the night, he'll feel dark, however dark it may be; when there's fog he'll feel foggy, however foggy it may be. I am certain that each individual becomes like his environment. But the environment, the surroundings, in a wider sense of the word, will not become like that individual, and that's what's interesting. The light doesn't become like the people who are looking at it; it is independent of them, and thereby autonomous.

Maybe the light is broken, but what does maybe mean. Maybe the light did glare at the surroundings after all. Then it broke into pieces. The light in this lake is just broken. But as I've told myself time and again, nothing is *like* anything. Nothing is like. Something that's *like* is neither this nor that.

3

Little Volatile Topography

JUST TO SET THINGS STRAIGHT: the word migration has nothing to do with Migros, the discount superstore. Migration means moving to a foreign country. But Migros is a foreign word of sorts as well, and one foreign word can remind you of another; anyway, in this case the mix-up is instructive, since it's always foreigners who migrate. Migraine.

Immigrants and emigrants are foreigners. When someone suddenly moves from one place to another and doesn't return to his original place for a while (which raises the question of how long a while is), he gradually takes on a disfigured look, and this is what we perceive as foreign.

As for me, I often spend a few years in each place, I'm always just passing through, I was in Vienna, Hamburg, Munich, back in Vienna, and I've now been in Switzerland for a while, but I will probably move on, meaning that I'm only here for the moment, which is different from setting out to alter your life once and for all, never to have to move on again. I am a transmigrant, and now I see the world-famous Alps every day, probably not forever. Everything I do,

I do daily, but I won't be doing it forever, and you can see that from my surroundings as a whole.

You can always tell things from someone's surroundings. You can also tell that someone's been away from home for a long time when he begins to lose his habits, or when he's already lost and forgotten them.

Habit is an important word when it comes to migration. The truly settled have settled into ways that those who wander are in a position to observe. Some wanderers travel only to watch the habits of the settled; they seek out such habits on their trips, and notice that these too are rooted in landscape. Mountain dwellers have strong lungs and go skiing, lake dwellers go for walks on the shore, and city dwellers avoid the streets by taking buses and subways.

In any case, even nowadays landscape is closely related to habits, and that's easiest to tell if you look at people who live fixed lives in a single place. It's harder to draw conclusions from observing migrants, which makes commenting on the differences between wanderers and the settled problematic.

Still, the settled are especially intriguing because there are hardly any of them left, everything and everyone is in flux, people can travel as much as they want. Then again, it wouldn't be accurate to call all those who like traveling migrants.

Nowadays, everyone is on their way somewhere, so the settled and the ultra-settled are in high demand. A settled person has inhabited one place for such a long time that it has become a proper habit.

The other one lost his face. He used to smile a lot,

having been taught how he ought to smile at home, but then he emigrated, he was young and learned otherwise. He acquired a serious expression, and after emigrating yet again, he arrived without it. In fact, he never really arrived in the second of his new environs. He claimed he understood people and responded to them, he was there, present, but remained inscrutable, as though he'd never actually arrived, and that was how he lost his face a second time.

Losing your face is highly characteristic of migrating. Looking in the mirror doesn't help when you're in a new place, nothing helps, no one approaches you, your own features are unfamiliar, initially to everyone else, and then gradually they become unfamiliar to you too.

Unlike the new arrival, another sort of personality is known beforehand; in which case, his features will have made an impression on everyone long before he arrives, making him a stranger who seems strange in a good way. There's a particularly good way of being unknown, which is not actually being unknown, but known, known for being unknown, and nearly everyone will always be interested in a stranger they already know.

To wander or to live. The word *wohnen*, "to live," used to mean something quite similar to *wandering*: it used to mean *searching*, in the sense of searching for nourishment. If the word had kept evolving and broadening itself, then perhaps it might now mean: to settle someplace, to live there, to live in a region or to live off it, to live together with others.

On that subject, living together must be practiced simul-taneously by everyone concerned. Of course any place will have someone who has lived or settled there for longer than the newcomer, that goes without saying, but still, in time they can all live together, the new and old wanderers and new and old settlers should stop keeping track of time. When a single person or a family or several families have only been settled in a given place for a few weeks and more people migrate to settle there as well, there won't be much trouble, unless there's not an inch of room left for the newcomers. But with time, earlier settlers develop habits, routes, and routines that make them feel that the place belongs to them and to no one else.

I used to love talking about emigrants and immigrants because it immediately reminded me of Beckett, Oscar Wilde, Gertrude Stein, Gombrowicz, Ödön von Horváth, and others, writers who didn't live in their country or even necessarily for their country, I decided that this was precisely what made them good writers, and I still think that.

Gombrowicz noted in his diary that as soon as someone is described as being English, French, or German, an image of this individual presents itself immediately and without any further elaboration, he could even appear as a character in a novel and be recognizable to the reader, whereas people from less well-known countries have to be described very carefully (or else they end up faceless). Observing migrants or portraying them in novels is significantly harder. What are migrants anyway!

They belong in every country as well as belonging to themselves, these delightful strangers, I thought. That made me feel pleased with my own history, I thought it would be good to belong more fully to Vienna and Hamburg and to other cities.

I know a French woman (a woman from a well-known country) who has lived in Germany for decades and can't seem to settle there happily. In this case it is *she* who can't forget where she is from, perhaps she won't want to forget for the next hundred years. Or three hundred years. Some people spend many centuries in another country but stay just as they were. Centuries are more or less a hundred years (according to Gertrude Stein), and a hundred years can't pass without any change. One hundred years is three generations and it's a terrible thing when nothing changes for a hundred years. It would be a terrible thing for the settled and the newcomers to be feuding still after a hundred years. Time is no trivial thing. No one would say it doesn't exist.

Or is there anyone who claims that there was only one decisive time, an unspecified ancient past in which everyone was assigned their particular place? But then the old order would have to be reestablished, everything would have to be tidied up, all the Germanic tribes would have to migrate together with the Slavic and Romansch tribes back to where they first came from, the Spanish and English would of course have to be fetched from America so that they could be returned home to their ancestral Indo-European home, the Hungarians would cross the Urals with the Finns back to the Altai Mountains, where, although the relationship between them has not been fully explained, they would meet the Japanese, and where the Eskimos would already be waiting. Everyone would be happy together, as they originally were, as if all that time they had been only transmigrants. But would they be ethnically organized? Or would they be herded hither and thither according to linguistic criteria? And who would have to be returned to which time period?

It is always instructive to discover someone's origins. Words are also like that; the past is interesting. To find out where someone is from is always fascinating, just as it's fascinating to learn where he is going. Why does someone keep drifting farther and farther away from his origins, what is it that's drawing him away, and where to? Where does he want to belong absolutely, and why?

I could move to Odessa or to Montreal right now, and what would happen then? If I had always wanted— wanted!—to move to Montreal or Madrid, where would I actually belong?

4

For

FOR US THE DRIVE BEGAN in Widen, *for* us, if that means anything, we were driving *for* the ride, for the sake of driving, from a hill in Widen we meandered along the road into a very wide valley; the road led the way, it knew how to descend into a valley like that over vast sweeping slopes, so we followed it. The vastness means we've come a long way. I have already decided—decided for myself, if that means anything—to follow every centimeter, every road and every fork, every route and detour, but it turns out that the roads and their forks are entangled, so deeply entangled that you can't go further along them bit by bit, ah, no, the road keeps unwinding in an Aargau way.

Just before we reach Bremgarten there's another huge billboard for that political party, and I try to avoid looking at it, having already managed to avoid looking in Widen; since I don't want to look at the announcement, I look past it into the landscape.

Driving further into Aargau, and

ah! Ah, Bremgarten is almost falling into the water, into the water, ah, the water, but there is no one along the Reuss for miles, so that the river almost swallows itself at the city bridge, in fact, are there fish in this river at all?

In Bremgarten I stumbled into the first pub and lingered for a while, I saw the silhouettes, generous lines arching over the—ah!—the river, the silhouette of the bridge, the riverbanks, the plummeting Reuss at 5 and even at 6 in the afternoon, although the roads do not want to be cut up into bits.

But there is nothing special about lingering in a pub, in consuming. And the desire to consume is conspicuous all over this country. On the road signs, the town of Widen is listed as Widen AG. Then Bremgarten. Then later there is Abtwil AG, and as we will later see, Buchs AG. Even some of the cars that drive through the country have AG on their license plates. People shouldn't simply succumb to this abundance of consumer options, or they might complain of not really having experienced enough and not being able to remember things. I drank the wine, looked at the Reuss, which wanted to plunge to its death, and thought about the ways in which consumption, profit, drinking wine, and driving onward are connected, and to make progress with my own experience, I asked the chubby waitress what the three stars fluttering on the Canton of Aargau's flag mean.

Ah, you should never ask about the stars. Or rather, whenever I want to ask about something I will. Beinwil, Uezwil, Abtwil, I *will* go to Baden and Aarau and to the mouths of these rivers because I want to. I want to travel further, and from that point on I hardly ever stay put in one place for as long as I did in Bremgarten; one day later, at the crossroads just before Windisch, at 11:40 in the morning, I saw Jonny Furrer's vacation-accident and made a note of the

time, while Jonny Furrer was standing on the roadside wearing tight swimming trunks and a bold orange vest, waving
down cars as they passed his crashed car, brandishing an
orange-red club in his hand and taking his time. I drove
further along, past him, I've come a long way.

We keep going, we're going on, to drive you have to be
driven, motivated, going forward, words like conducting
and directing are all related to the act of driving, all related
to the question of *for*,

and ah, water again, now it's pouring down, hailstones
falling from a yellow sky, Aargau, a wild country, in Abtwil
trees fell directly across my path, but I was protected and
am still alive, the next day I drive north again, again with
this same feeling,

ah, ah, water, through Aristau and past it, now, in this
moment, water, that is to say the thing flowing by right now,

and what is a river valley? It's a field!

I would like best of all to be able to house all of Aargau
in a single word, devour the whole canton in a single word,
ah, there, where the Reuss flows into the Aare and keeps
going, or at any rate, where the Aare gulps the Reuss down,
a great wet gulp, it was really hot, but they've made it difficult to look at that swallowing, made it difficult for me, and
all the more I think that people must consider it unchaste
to look, if that means anything, that is to say, the others
consider it salacious to look at rivers, and that's why they put
forests at the mouths of rivers, whereas I want to look at the
mouths of rivers, to look them in the mouth, which would
be like putting all of Aargau in a single word, devouring

a whole canton in a single word, oh there, words in the mouth, names that will keep, that can be kept, that lie in the mouth every now and again, the Aare, the Reuss, and how the Limmat flows into the Aare and onwards, again it was really hot, but they made it difficult to see the gulp, as though precisely this type of seeing were unchaste.

Word inventory at 4:10 in the afternoon: most importantly, *for. Fork, forget, forward, field, water,* and *consumption.* And *drive,* which has to be the first thing you need, at least for *driving.* At any rate, in Aargau words lie in your mouth for a long time, and it turns out that even this is related to the rivers; many words can no longer be forgotten along the Aare, for many centuries people have forgotten to forget them, and words make you think about the past.

As a result, I drove to Habsburg. I hadn't driven there earlier, I was driving there now, to Habsburg, which was once called Habichtsburg. The village has declined economically, who'd have thought that they'd serve breaded pig's neck in the place where the House of Habsburg originated, even the castles (not just the roads) show you something; the castle showed me how to look into the landscape so that I suddenly became distinctly tall, with my head up in the air, the castle looked into the distance with a certain sense of being surrounded by hills, we'd come a long way, the castle had a sense of elevation that means something.

Aargau contains the word *Gau,* the Nazi term for a region. Rejecting the word *Gau* is not unheard of today. I wonder who would want to keep what words in his mouth, and whether someone else could maybe tell what he had in his mouth; or rather, I mean you can tell what almost anyone is thinking, you can tell what I'm thinking, and to make sure no one looks me in the mouth, I shake my head and drive on.

A road doesn't just come to an end, it goes on endlessly, a road is not allowed to give up unexpectedly for no apparent reason, but it would be even worse for a river to freeze midstream than for a road to stop at random. It would be more obvious if a river stopped flowing than if a road stopped. Because a road doesn't flow, it runs and goes places. But there is one thing that both roads and rivers do. They rush. Onward, forward, for, ford.

You're standing by the river just staring into space—look, the water surprises you.

The water, yes the water, what else but the water, why. I drove from Aarau to Baden and to Windisch, from there to Brugg, and the Reuss had already joined the Aare and would lead northward, draining north all the way to the Rhine.

There I saw someone who was a stranger to me, but whom I was meeting for the second time, he got out of his car and said, like he had said the first time: You're standing by the river just staring into space.

These are public waters, I wanted to say, but he had already gotten into his car and driven away, I didn't even get a chance to ask him about the stars.

And someone told me that I should go to Muri, that I would like it there, and someone else said I should go to Mellingen, but in Mellingen I found only a beauty that was private to the person who had told me about the place, it was nine and I had just had breakfast,

and whether someone's breakfast is really public or private is an open question, breakfast might seem to be a private matter, but when someone's personal breakfast equips him for the day and hence for other people, then his morning meal is not entirely private, and the previous night, while he was sleeping, he will already have been fortified so as to have the strength to go through the day (or drive through it, rather!), for other people and hence publicly, in which case if someone sleeps for other people and eats for them the next morning, everything he does is public, I thought, which suggests that I was not entirely myself, if that means anything, or rather I mean that I was not with myself, nor was I with other people, but I could not get rid of the impression that I had penetrated public privacy, even if only early in the morning, that's what a country, a *Geaue*, a canton is like. Somehow the people in a canton ultimately belong together, both in the morning and at night, that isn't anything special, and perhaps I will reflect on this phenomenon again tonight.

And the Aare is lonely even in Aarau, whereas I read somewhere that before getting there the young river is impetuous, I read somewhere, impetuous, before arriving in Aargau, and then it arrives, is constantly, constantly arriving, it bursts through the border to Aargau and I see, ah, the water is full of pebbles, debris, it expands—we've come a long way—and promptly drops, becomes slower, hides in the forest and flows out of it, now that is something special, and we are standing down by the river.

In the meantime Aarau stays put. I mean, it's hard for a city to lead out of itself, and ultimately it's proud of the fact that it doesn't lead out of itself and instead stays put in the same place for a long time. Aarau has been taking place in Aarau for a long time, even though Rheinfelden may be significantly older, Rheinfelden, which has been inhabited for seven thousand years, or rather someone, note, someone lived there seven thousand years ago and did not live there alone.

No, in that case I will not cede myself to the city, nor to the rushing water in Aarau, which swallows itself, which discretely swallows itself in loneliness, in plunging. Of course sometimes I was lonelier when traveling with a companion than alone, and it can be revealing to observe whether someone is driving through the network alone or with a companion, through the network of the vast, wet land, along the river. People even came in legions from the south and went as far as the Rhine. Groups of them often settled there, leaving traces, in that the paths learned certain directions from the people or they from the paths, and then they would go on further, fork, double in number after the forks and lead even further, and that's how I mixed up the contours of time, lost the silhouettes over the ah, the Aare,

but not all places are built near the water, not at all.

Sometimes the river is hidden, and new stations that have been built near the water also lie hidden, they are power stations, and only the fields are visible, wet river valleys often covered with deciduous forest, lowlands, fields, whereas even the direction of travel is intriguing, that is to say, whether someone is on the road alone or in the company of several people in a north–south direction, or whether the rivers flow south–north, out toward the north, out of the country, always with the fields in between.

In between I simply look into the sky, past the billboards, and at the junction between Muri and Beinwil, I even try to overlook a big signboard, because I read the phrase *workers' colony* on the sign, and it's all too easy to reject that phrase nowadays.

Besides, the swift streets are immediately visible to everyone. An automobile driver stops on the side of the street, or perhaps a little further on, he has to find out alone, *auto*, by himself, where he's meant to drive to, he's looking, and then he drives for himself, for his own drive, and drives on, that happens quite often, that's what the roads are there for, roads often exist where something can be found, which was how I would reach Hallwil and Alliswil via Aabach, by willing to get there. I wanted to so much! I wanted to put everything in a single word, to look that word in the mouth, to look the Reuss and the Aare in their mouths, ah, the water, yes, where the Reuss flows into the Aare and keeps flowing, onwards, where the Aare swallows the Reuss, it's a great wet gulp, but they make it difficult to see this swallowing, as though precisely this type of seeing were unchaste.

Huge mosquitoes were stinging me at the hidden mouth of the Reuss. Furthermore, the Reuss always flows wildly, swiftly, in isolation, plunging secretly and under military oversight into the Aare, and then hurrying on, not that anyone sees it, it can only be seen in the woods, where it comes out of hiding, as I was hoping to be able to look at both of them, the Aare and the Reuss, to see how they had actually met, a war started, I was an intruder, there goes the intruder, they hissed, they rushed at me, stung me at once, and as I ran from the forest seething with anger, because I wasn't going to just let them sting me and was going to stop looking for mouths of rivers, they followed me outside of their sovereign jurisdiction. Those sticky mosquitoes.

You're standing by the river just staring into space, someone could well say right now.

The Aare later became somewhat intimidated when it reached the Rhine, and at the Rhine the embarrassing, isolated past of its history was over, people came in boats and went swimming.

Word inventory at 11:20: *For*, and more importantly, *forward*, *forward*, the fields were wet depressions in the earth, and hopefully there will soon be only one word left.

Jonny Furrer's vacation-accident would soon take place between Buchs and Suhr.

He stood on the road in a pair of long swimming trunks, had thrown on an orange safety vest, using a club that could hardly be overlooked to wave the cars that had not yet been in accidents past his crashed vacation car, but I had to go on to Zofingen; before then, ah, the cross shape of a plane appeared above Buchs, it flew in a straight line for a while, and then it was about to nosedive forward, and then the big cross flew with its nose pointing upwards, then the plane spun on its own axis while flying, and finally I looked upwards, the air was filled with today's Aargau, I looked up to the airplane, to this somewhat impersonal invitation into the air, an impersonal but almost private idea in public, again the plane seemed to nosedive, to plummet forward, I had almost forgotten about driving, about driving on, about driving for the roads, in an Aargau way, against the direction of the river's course. Who was opposed to whom?

Then I stepped out onto a garden terrace, all that with Buchs AG and the abundance of consumer options was over, I sat in the countryside with a glass of wine and thought about how much I had always liked the word *for*, forward along the forks, and whether the word could lead me any further. So I eventually drove through the fields into Zofingen, at 5 in the evening; that is certainly the best time to arrive in Zofingen.

And the word inventory at this time: ah for rivers, and for driving on.

5

Elevation Gain

THE MOUNTAINSIDE ADVANCING toward me will either swallow my voice or send it ricocheting back. If the latter, it'll double or quadruple my voice, and since it's getting closer and closer, I keep quiet for a while to play it safe.

For years I have wanted to see things as they are, to stop trying to compare every single thing with something familiar.

The mountain range is actually the mountain range, the mountain is the mountain, the hill is the hill and nothing else, there's no need to blush, no double meaning.

The valley is truly a valley. I love looking down at it. For almost an hour I have been taking the cable car from Celerina up to Marguns and back again, and when I look around, I can see that I'm traveling.

Up until now I've never made an effort to hear something the way I make an effort to see it. Of course it sometimes happened that I was listening correctly, but I'd never made a real effort to do so, sometimes I would succeed without trying, without realizing that I had succeeded, and now, in the cable car, I'm more or less shut off, I can only hear cowbells ringing on the hillside beneath me, and I ask myself, here in a landscape that is as foreign to me as it ever was, what happens to voices in mountains.

The mountainside advancing toward me could absorb my voice. But if it sends it ricocheting back, my voice will be doubled or quadrupled.

When I got here a week ago, Herta was standing in front of the house where I am living right now, she greeted me right then, that afternoon she greeted me again, and the third time I saw her, she gave me three kisses or air kisses on the left and right and left cheeks, and we spoke briefly.

The next day I asked her if she would be traveling often and how her summer was going, and she answered both questions with a drawn-out *Yeahhhhh*.

I asked her if it was dangerous to travel by cable car in this weather, and she said *yes*, her voice first starting the word on a high note before deepening, then getting much lower than it had started but not very low, and finally climbing again, I hardly understood her drawn-out, swallowed-up, tripartite *yes*.

A sound is a sound, and you could even say: a sound is a sound is a sound is a sound. Which is not to say that a sound is nothing, but a sound, and that's all there is to it.

For instance, a sound is a sound because it sounds from all sides. To someone who's standing up front compared to someone who's in the back, the sound that remains a sound sounds different. It stays the same but is perceived differently.

Someone who is very far away from a sound probably won't hear what he could hear up close, which is why it is worth saying that a sound is a sound, and it makes a difference who is talking where and with what kind of voice.

Who, where, and with what kind of voice: that is why speech hinges on landscape, and sound hinges on environment. Language in the Alps also hinges on the Alps.

Herta lives in one of the neighboring mountain valleys, and in the evenings she likes to look southward. She sits down, lets her hands fall in her lap, and gazes toward the south, in the west the sun is setting.

Meanwhile I have learned that her name is not Herta but Berta, Herta has always been a misunderstanding, a name based fundamentally on a misunderstanding, and many misunderstandings can eventually be associated with various landscapes.

Herta's real name is Berta, but another man who lives around here asked me emphatically not to call her Berta.

Well then what? I asked.

Just call her *she*, he said.

But I did not like the idea of just calling her *she*, like saying *that woman there*, so the best solution seemed to be calling her Herta instead of Berta.

Five days ago I visited her at home for the first time, the sun was setting in the west, we sat down, and I told her one of the stories I had read about the Alps.

She told me other such stories, and as long as we were sitting there together, all was well. She spoke unhurriedly, and as she spoke she shook her blond hair slowly, as if she were from a distant past. Eventually I too tried to speak more slowly so that she would understand me better. She had ten tones, her words went up and down, and it seemed to me that I only had three or four tones.

I once asked her whether she noticed that too, and she said *Yeahhhhh*.

She said it twice, that long, drawn-out, despairing word.

Ayayayay, culomba,
there's no need to cry.

Ch'üna culomba trista
la daman bodezzas ha
cumanzâ a chantar
illa chasetta solitaria
cun las portas spalancadas.

I have since gone up to see her a few times, and she always greets me with three kisses. Then we both look around and look silently into the rocks, looking up into the rocky cliff face.

At some point Gian came up the mountain and greeted us with a curt nod, and I said I already knew a few people around there. Then we drove together to a nearby village where seven languages were spoken. There they told me about other villages in that area with ten or twelve different languages.

Or maybe they were saying something altogether different and I misunderstood, I could only ever make out single words, words from ten or twelve languages.

The languages had fallen down the rock walls and shattered and were almost unintelligible, even though people didn't speak quickly. Even though people were cautious and proceeded slowly, the languages crashed to the ground.

The speed of speech is interesting and yet people hardly talk about it, you could also talk about tempo, every language has a base tempo quite separate from its words, and going quickly or slowly or in between or changing speeds are among the possibilities it offers. How quickly something is said and in what tone of voice, that's another story.

I've been told that languages need to be apprehended above the diaphragm, and that is probably where they are apprehended even now, except that no one talks much about the diaphragm anymore.

I think people use their heads to understand the meanings of words, regardless of how they are spelled, whereas they use their diaphragms to understand the speed and sound of the words, and use both to understand the meaning. You have to breathe in deeply.

But because tones are perceived differently from different angles, it makes a difference who speaks how and how quickly, which is how languages end up being shaped by landscape, by topography.

The scene inside the cable car consists of two rows of seats facing each other, surrounded by the view, artfully curved metal bars between the viewing windows, other metal fittings, including the metal built into the floor, and there's a deaf humming all around me. I am being carried upwards, roughly northwards, I have already climbed two hundred meters above ground, or rather, I've been carried, there are five hundred and sixty meters between the lower and the upper terminals, which I barely notice even though I want to pay special attention to the sensation of height, but

I keep getting distracted, right now I'm flying over a clump of fir trees, I switch on my tape recorder and tell myself that I'm flying over some fir trees and have an all-day pass; I could stay in the car until night falls if I like. Someone else is going up and down in another cable car, Pierre, but I don't know how long he's staying and what he's looking at, we haven't made any plans apart from having dinner together.

When someone reaches the upper cable car terminal, he won't necessarily get the impression of being at a great height. He might, but only at first glance. Later, he'll think he could go even further up the tall mountains. When he looks around, he'll see the view only when he looks south, because the mountains are blocking the view north, and then he'll keep going.

A UFO is coming toward me, it's coming right at me and going past me into the valley, and this cable car flying toward me seems faster than my own. In my cabin I can hear a humming noise, here I can go on talking without being disturbed, and simply forget about the rock walls and the question of whether they swallow up sound.

Before I boarded the cable car, I thought hard about not wanting to be here on foot, not among the rocks, where no one would hear me if I screamed for ages. In certain spots I might get lucky, someone might notify the *Rega*, who would send a rescue helicopter, but then I would have to be prepared, I'd have to know how to shout for help around here if you want to be heard.

O and U sounds don't work, I take it.

If you were to cry *Look up!* no one would hear you.

It would be pointless to hide in a crevice waiting for help

and screaming *Done for, dead of cold*, because it would be almost *soundless*.

A and I are probably the right sounds, the ones I would have to shout out, practically sing out.

I keep imagining crevices like that, chasms, slippery hillsides; on the mountain I keep noticing how you could fall off the edge.

I should have asked Herta days ago how to talk when it's windy, when it's five on the Beaufort scale, for instance. And whether I should lower my voice when talking over the Alpine foehn wind. And whether I should use a metronome to practice this slower tempo of speech.

Yesterday I jotted down a few key words, took my umbrella with me, and went to see her. I read her my questions, and she answered with her drawn-out, tripartite *Yeahhhhh*, which might have been an actual answer.

Then she said she wanted to tell me something.

Once, with a few friends, she had chipped off the surface of a cliff face, and a word jutted out: CRAP.

CRAP means something like *stone* in pre-Roman languages. Together they took their find to Chur and received eighty francs for it. Since then, CRAP has lain in an airtight room, no one has done more research on it, but anyone can visit it.

What does pre-Roman mean, I ask.

Yeahhhhh, she said. As though she didn't trust me.

I said: people say that on winter nights around New Year's, at the witching hour, a man with a flowing cloak and wide-brimmed hat appears in the woods on a hill near here, riding a white horse. When asked who he is, he doesn't answer, and rides off into the storm.

Herta nodded.

I said: Where the huge Bernina glaciers lie today, there used to be a vast alpine pasture full of flowers.

Herta nodded.

The pasture belonged to a miser called Rospo, who is said to have been as ugly as a toad.

Is said to have been? she asked.

Is said to have been.

One day, a beggar came by, and Rospo didn't want to give him any food, although he himself took pleasure in always eating well. But his servant took pity on the beggar and fed him generously, and the beggar advised him to flee immediately because there was a disaster at hand. That night, dark clouds climbed above the pasture, which is to say above the alp, and it soon began to snow. The next morning, right where the miser's pastures had been, the Bernina glaciers had formed. Rospo grew cold, and he called out to his dog, Morina, asking her to come and warm his feet. He has been calling to her since then, in vain.

That's a dog's tale, I said.

No it's not, said Herta, and of course she knew the story much better than I did.

Then I told her everything else I was reading or had read or have read. Time is tricky, the past is past, and it's just like a sound or the view. The view looks different from different angles, and that's what the past is like.

Depending on whether you are looking at it sideways, from beneath or from above, it looks different, although it is still the past, and that's what mountain peaks are like. From one side they seem near to you, and then they seem more distant, and the same is true of the past.

I read, I have read, perhaps it is best to say:

Ten years ago, I read the following story about a wild man:

In the forests near here lived *Omo Selvatico*, the wild man. The old farmers say that anything he said was well said. So do you know what he did when the weather was bad? He laughed. And one day, someone who happened to see him asked why he was laughing. Ah, he said, I'm laughing because something good always comes after something bad. When the sun is shining, I'll cry.

There is also a story to the contrary, Herta said.

I know, I said. The contrary story would be:

Frau Berta was a wild woman who lived in a cave with her husband, the wild man (*L'om Salvedgh*). She protected all the good families and was particularly generous to those who honored and venerated her and did not arouse her wrath. But woe to those who offended her by treating her with contempt! Nothing good would come to them; even their best cows would stop producing milk.

Herta nodded, but she had been anticipating a different story. She wanted to talk about Gian.

I güran cha quista
culomba
nu saja nügl'oter
co sia orma,
Ayayayay, culomba!

A man who lives around here had translated this song from the Spanish. I met him a few weeks ago, when I first came to Celerina to look at cable cars, and although I hardly knew him, he told me he was always happy to bring any conceivable song from Spanish over into Romansch, the fact that there were mountains there and mountains here was a good enough reason to translate them, the songs would like it here, but to begin with he would need a German version, just to be safe. So I got hold of the exact wording of the songs and translated them into German, and then he actually translated three songs, we're going to keep doing this, even if the process is somewhat laborious, until the two not too distant languages grow closer, and Pierre shook his head at the thought of how laborious this was, or rather he chuckled to himself.

In a flat landscape, the voice travels serenely, it goes away, further away, and gets lost. The mountains, on the other hand, swallow up the voices, bouncing some of them back and altering others, jagged, rocky, sandy, domed, forested, grassy, and stony mountains all play with sounds differently, and this playing makes the mountains instruments.

It can also happen that a sound gets caught in the mountains and never stops sounding, and can consequently be heard five days or a week or even a year later.

Gian came down the slope, and Herta waved at him. While we were waiting for him, she talked about his vitality, and especially the astonishing vitality of his language. She never talked about liveliness, always about vitality, and she kept repeating the word.

Then Gian came to us and showed us the different mountain groups. He pointed out all the valleys by name, and said
that onomastics, the study of names, was very important
to him. There is a shared past hidden in names, he said,
particularly in how you can sound out traces of pre-Roman
history from them.

Pre-Roman times? I asked.

Exactly. Words like CRAP and GONDA. Individual
locales were divided from one another many times over, he
explained, often by obstacles such as mountain ranges and
canyons, which caused them to develop separately. Anyway,
it's still too early to say anything definitive on this question,
he said.

I had the impression that he had already told me this
once with the same words, but in any case he spoke German
to me, and I would hardly have understood him otherwise.

When he got up to leave and Herta became quiet and
dejected, I called out:

Culomba!

Nu cridar tuottüna plü!

At noon today I met up with the man who translates
Spanish songs. We sat on the terrace of an Italian restaurant,
and he tried to teach me how to pronounce the word *chi so*,
which means the same thing as the Spanish *quizás*. Over
coffee, I asked him how the beautiful Italian language can
be put into Romansch. Oh, he said, you have to make very
careful distinctions.

A sound is a sound and is different from different angles.
If you're hearing it from the south, everything will sound

different from how it sounds when someone from the north suddenly arrives and hears the sound of the words, and of the summer rain.

It's been raining in the meantime, around the upper terminal the stony ground is yellow, the meadows are well trodden, dried out, turned into steppe, rain does some good, and when someone comes from the north, even the smell of the rain and the sound it makes seems southern, and because a sound sounds different from different angles, it makes a difference who is speaking where and in what voice. You have to know all the respective places well.

A UFO comes toward me again, suddenly the cable car shoots out of the lower terminal and comes right at me, I, in contrast, have almost reached the bottom, and I arrive in the blue hall in Celerina for the seventh time today. There the cabin moves slowly along. I could get out, someone else could get on, and he could get out again twelve minutes later, up on the mountain, and go on by foot, but I stay put, I and my cabin will be moved along slowly, like all the other cabins, bit by bit, and at just the right moment we will be thrust out of the terminal.

The cowbells can be heard even from within the enclosed cabin, and after I have rewound the tape recorder to check a few sentences, there they are on the tape again, and I can see, or rather hear that I have not made any notes on the southern view, or on the descent. My voice disappears from the tape at regular intervals because it gets swallowed up whenever the cabin passes one of the huge poles. At the poles the cabin always jiggles slightly, I wonder for a moment whether the car will keep going, and then it's quiet except for a low drone.

I have been visiting Herta in her valley almost every evening until now, and since I found out that her name is actually Berta, I haven't used her name at all, so as not to misspeak.

Once we both sat, silently, in front of her house, the sun was setting in the west, we were both looking up silently at the rock cliff, and partway into this silence she said her long, drawn-out *Yeahhhh*.

Culomba nu cridar
tuottüna plü!

When Gian joined us, we drove to a nearby village that spoke many languages, which had all had broken off from each other and fallen off the cliff. *Chi so, chi so.*

The upper terminal is made of iron and painted a bright red that's almost pink, which makes it look like a garage, although neither it nor the lower terminal is one, and it really shouldn't look like one if it isn't, but all that iron and the employees in mechanics' uniforms who won't look you in the eye because they are doing their jobs, all that reminds you of a garage.

The reason why they don't look at me is because I'm not getting out, although they could also approach me precisely for that reason, while my cabin is being inched along toward the descent. They could offer me a coffee or ice cream, they sell ice cream even in winter, when all the cable cars available are mounted and occupied, besides, they could tell me that they're always full on days with plenty of snow. Or they could tell me that Pierre, the other cable car rider who hasn't gotten out yet, is taking a break right now, drinking coffee. But I, for my part, am not asking them for news of this other person.

Recently, above Marguns, a man fell and landed in a ravine, no one heard his cries, and they found him days later, frozen into ice, not far off grew an edelweiss flower, and a chamois had also sprung around up there.

Ch'üna culomba trista la daman bodezzas ha cumanzâ a chantar . . .

Before I got into the cable car after lunch, I thought for a while about the fact that if anything were to happen to me here in the rocks and gorges, I could shout for ages and no one would hear me, because I wouldn't know how to go about shouting in these parts.

I doubt anyone would hear me. In certain spots I might be lucky, someone might notify the *Rega*, who would send a rescue helicopter.

Once I got out of a bus in the mountains with a stranger, it was a mail van, we went a few steps up the snow-covered mountain, and the man said, you have to go uphill slowly.

The same applies to the speed of speech.

I jotted down several key words, took my umbrella, and went to see Herta, to read her the questions that she answered with her drawn-out *Yeahhhhh*. Then she told me that she had once found the word CRAP jutting out of the rock, CRAP means something like stone, I could see it in Chur if I wanted to, a pre-Roman word.

What do you mean by that, I asked.

Yeahhh, she said, as though she didn't trust me.

She always kissed me and then refused to explain anything.

To distract her, I talked about the Bernina glaciers. There used to be a great, blooming pasture there, an alp. She nodded.

The pasture belonged to a miser called Rospo.

The Rospo, not Rospo, Herta said, but there are other interesting stories, she said, looking me in the eyes.

I said: Frau Berta was a wild woman, but there was not just one, but many Frau Bertas, and people believed that when women were alone at night without their men, evil things could happen to them. Woe to those to whom *the* Frau Bertas appeared. One night twelve women sat spinning, the clock struck eleven, and one of them remarked: There are no men among us today, let us go, or disaster will befall us. She had scarcely spoken these words when there was a knocking at the door, and it was the Frau Bertas.

Herta would have preferred to talk about Gian, but she always let me talk about what I wanted, as long as it was her stories I told. She let me tell her stories she knew, her own stories, and never asked about any other stories, or rather she never asked anything.

In flat, open terrain, voices can only gradually get lost, I said.

But by then she was deep in her own thoughts.

The cable car is starting to travel upwards again, toward the mountain range, toward a broad rock face that gives the impression that there isn't anything behind it. The upper terminal lies beneath it, which is why no one who gets out of a cable car gets the impression of being at a great height, it's certainly the case that he can go even further up and reach the top, and when he's on top of the rock face, he can call downwards, hurling his own voice down.

A UFO is coming toward me again, the still, muffled thing is coming at me almost horizontally, it goes past me, both cabins are now in a mountain valley, I will keep going upward, never very steeply, and between the slopes lie large, flat fields. The fields and the slopes are yellow, and there are stones of every size. Nearly all the cabins are empty, rain shimmers outside at the windows, and you can't recognize anyone, not even inside the occupied cabins.

Gian points from Herta's house to the different mountain groups, calls the valleys by their names and says: Half the past lies in these names. He especially wants to emphasize the words CRAP and GREP.

Never again will I forget these words.

GONDA means a pile of rocks, he explains, but the different locales have been separated from one another by all kinds of tricky obstacles, which mean they are more likely to develop separately.

Gradually, it seemed like he was no longer talking to me, but to a remote circle of listeners, to many people, and that he was capable neither of whispering nor of murmuring. He is always shouting, like an orator, like he's talking into a broken microphone.

When someone hurts his head, it helps to talk to him during the first few moments, and not speak too softly, so that the injured person realizes that someone is counting on him and needs him. You have to tell him that to make sure he doesn't crawl into himself and fall asleep. You can't speak to an injured person in a whisper. Gian always talks as though someone has fallen and hurt himself. He's gotten used to talking at the top of his voice.

After he left, Herta said that he'd come by way of Bärenstraße, and then she became so sad that her sentences nearly lost their singsong tone.

Culomba, the weeping in the mountains.

Herta reminded me of someone when she spoke, and so did Gian. It's likely that every voice reminds you of another voice, and being able to recognize languages is also an art, recognizing the sound of voices, which only partly belong to you yourself, and will always remind someone of something else.

But we have not even gotten to the chamois, its tremendous tempo and appalling silence, what people used to call a deafening silence.

When I describe it to myself and look down into the valley, I harden into a salt column.

Culoma, nu cridar tuottüna plü!

6

Don't Say Anything

IT'LL BE AN ETERNITY before all the words that exist have been put away. Put away, so that every single word—you'll just have to imagine how many there are—so that each one of them can be seen from every angle, allowing everyone to see where it's from, what it wants to say, what it isn't saying because it simply can't, or because its tongue was torn out, no, that's too vivid, because its mind was damaged, some words end up with an interrupted mind, whereas others never do. Some words continue sparkling forever without suffering greatly. The word *Auge* or eye, for instance, is very old, a beautiful word, and it has simply remained as it is, without breaking, which is why it's with your *Augen* that you see. Apart from the eyes, the whole body, or nearly all of it, has kept well, the arms, legs, and mouth are called what they've always been called, although the *Beine* or legs will have to tell their curious story (not that they do, no one talks about the past), but wine, or rather the word *Wein*, was once a foreign word before it settled into German, and the words *Tulpe* (tulip) and *Rose* have settled right in, not just symbolically, but in the thick of the action, so much so that they don't sound foreign at all, despite having once been foreign words. Curiously, many plant names are impenetrable, so to

61

speak, and someone should explain why plants in particular are so often given foreign names. As though plants, of all things, were the ones that had something to hide, *roses*, *lilies*, *gladiolus flowers*, as though there were more to conceal about them than about one's own body.

As for me, I would like to be able to tell where words are from by just looking at them, because I must admit that I don't just speak, I speak with words, with the help of words.

That was what I wanted to talk about yesterday, I was giving a small lecture and had a speech prepared. The listeners arrived before the lecture started, ready to listen to the speech, having consented to be introduced to the words that they tossed around so frequently. Weapons (spears) are being flung about all the time, you could bundle them up and take them to market, to the farmer's market, or toss them around there, people do that too. Or is the word bazaar better than market? Do we live in a bazaar economy? Do we go to super-bazaars to prop up the economy? But to return to the word *throw*: the words *warp*, *reject*, and *hyperbole* all used to mean *throw*, imagine that. And to return to the listeners: many of them knew each other, there was plenty of hugging and kissing, and they said, you look good, I guess you look good, you look great, or: Mr. So-and-so, you look great today, or you're looking good today, better yet, don't you look great today, you look so young, they glide further along, past each other, and a few steps later they'll say: you look good, you're looking great today.

7

Pelican

THE CAR STOPPED ONLY BRIEFLY, and he leaped out and began to run, which he was good at. He was about thirty, tall, not too tall, and clearly pleased with himself. While he was running, he only liked himself for the first three hundred meters or so, and then he turned into a side street and disappeared. A few moments earlier, a light had come on in the house across the road and a naked man had appeared at the window, younger than the first, you could tell he was hungry, which was a pleasant sight as long as the hungry man remained calm. He looked down onto the street—certainly no one would see him from there. A drunk has been standing next to our door for days with a bottle in his hand, he just stands there blearily, drinking with his eyes closed. The naked man saw neither the drunk nor me. Then Joe came to the door with his head hanging down and rang the bell. He climbed the stairs. When he came in, he laid his head on my shoulder.

Joe is a pelican. People say he's a stork, but despite his mutability he isn't one, although he's often mistaken for one. Pelicans awake twice a year and are almost completely melancholy, I say *melancholy* because he would become even more despondent if someone called him dejected. He is actually dejected, but then he gets over it and takes flight, making loud noises as he flies, lands before long, and says that more than anything he would like to look disheveled. He is not hungry. He doesn't like it when anyone talks about how little appetite he has. As soon as he notices that he isn't suffering from hunger, he begins to worry that I might reproach him, and immediately he lays his head on my shoulder, and then I put my arms around his head. That's fine, I could deal with that for hours. But after twenty-four hours, at the very latest, I begin to argue with him, gradually at first, first of all I explain that I am not a pelican, and then I say softly that I will become melancholy if I have to act as if I am melancholy, at which he lets both his great wings fall in a way I have never seen any other bird do, as if he wanted to shake them out like a dusty or grimy coverlet, his head twitches, I'm taking cover, I've had it with you and your impatience, he says.

This time his feathers were gummed up with grease, and he couldn't clean them because he'd injured his bill two days ago, he kept shaking his wings out slowly but it didn't help, and there really was no reason to be happy. I reassured him that he didn't have fleas and told him that his feet were fine, only his claws needed a trim, which meant I'd have to trim them for him, since he can't see all the way down to his feet, he can't remember the last time he was able to see himself in a mirror, nor can I, since there aren't any more mirrors or windowpanes. Anti-glare glass has been installed in nearly all the windows, and the rest have wooden or iron shutters. This must have been why the man in the house opposite ours was standing in front of the open window, because the presence of another person works like a mirror, and when you don't have that option, you have to find a replacement. I, for instance, only ever see snippets of myself, I never see my back, and sometimes I look at my legs and find a run in my tights. I have runs in my tights, therefore I am.

We should really eat something, Joe said, dragging himself to the kitchen. On the street, three policemen were running toward the train station brandishing beaming flashlights. Joe said that didn't interest him, he had a meter-long neck ache, and his only remaining thought was that he wanted to eat something, but he didn't want to tell me what pelicans like having. In fact, I've never seen what he eats, what he scarfs down as soon as he's left the apartment and is alone. He doesn't fly when he's leaving, he goes down the stairs and closes the door behind him.

When he got outside he spoke to the drunk, but as far as I could tell, the drunk ignored him. Anyway, there are lights in the streets again, lights wavering slipshod, cars going places. Someone just stopped and tossed some books out of their car onto the pavement, bundles of paper, crumpled envelopes, there were probably letters in them too.

8

Winter

SEVERAL HUNDRED PEOPLE were waiting in a great hall when the door opened and a man came in, the last one, so to speak, the one who arrived last, which means something. Actually being last isn't easy. The people stood facing each other in two long rows, waiting, and the man walked between them, first nodding wordlessly to the left and to the right, then striding forward, holding his head high, it all came down to holding his head high. His forehead gleamed, he had big, wide-open eyes, which you could see even in profile, his nose gleamed too, or rather, his head was very round, very polished, if you looked more closely at the back of his head, it was bald and also gleaming, and as he strode forward you could see from every angle that his skin was gleaming, or rather: it was not really a head that the man carried on his shoulders, but a radiance, a penetrating glow that shone through everything; the head threw light on the other heads and figures around it, more and more light, and everyone could see with increasing clarity that a lightbulb was glowing where his head should have been, everywhere he went lit up, and as he reached the back of the long room, someone said cheers, glasses clinked, and someone else called out, the lightbulb just broke.

Helmut Heißenbüttel told me about the lightbulb a man carried as his head, he was astonished that this was even possible, but something similar had once happened to me. I stood in front of a door concealed by wallpaper, and when I opened it I found myself striding into a large hall, left and right of the door stood many people facing each other in two rows, and while I walked along between them, I could feel my skin becoming thinner and probably gleaming, I had beads of sweat on my forehead, on my nose, and on the back of my head, and I knew without even having to touch my head that it was turning into glass. I could see through my own glass and I saw at once that all the other heads had turned into lightbulbs. Then the light gradually became so bright that I couldn't see anything, and someone called out cheers.

These days it gets dark early, at a quarter past five in Lugano, at five here in Basel, by four-thirty in Hamburg, further north the night begins at midday, and from then on everything is always artificially lit. The less daylight there is, the more important lights and candles become. The smallest fire sparks wonder, a matchstick, a smoldering cigarette. Blue and yellow lights give the place a particular tone, but the most important color is red.

Here, night falls at five in the evening, and from then on everything is lit in red, the red tint of winter is reflected in the puddles, red is warm, warming, festive, cozy, familiar, trustworthy, attractive, romantic, invigorating, bracing, promising, and full of memories. Not to mention that the color red has something reckless about it.

Red is the color of courage, and whether it's courageous or not, red is always provocative,

now you're thinking about something that I didn't mention but am also thinking about,

who wouldn't,

we don't have to compete with each other,

it's all the same which one of us was the first to think that thought,

why should we have to compete,

on my account you've been thinking about nothing else this whole time, which says something,

in any case we can now see dark-red lips, naturally in a house that's glowing bright red, and nearby three pastry shops have had to close down. A hostile takeover, that's what they called it. It would stimulate growth in the red-light district. The chocolate scene is dead, twenty-three jobs were lost, and a few of the sales clerks went over to the other side, they were probably hostile to begin with. Instead of the candy stores there are entire houses full of red lamps, and in the middle of the night, the winter night, red-lipped, red-eyed women in red boots and red underwear emerge from the houses and breathe red fire.

A man with a white beard unbuttons his long red coat, discards his beard, and hurries naked into the house, that's how it goes! he screams, why on earth,

I am not going to figure the world out or see through it, not even in winter, and I am not pretending to be happy about it, which is to say that I'm not pretending to be happy about how the color red is abused under these or any circumstances at all. *(Coughing)* How did I end up here? Great, if I've lost my good mood I've lost everything, that much is clear, there's always something that's forbidden, and right now losing your good mood is forbidden, that is what the sales clerks at the candy stores told me too.

Show your teeth, they said,

but then there'll be black ravens flying past,

did you think about that? Have you had to imagine everything on your own? Why didn't you say anything?

Ravens used to be called firebirds because they love smoke and always have. They can even start fires on their own, they love to set things on fire, they still fly past smoky fires and screech, pause, and screech again, the various meanings of the color red are all the same to them!

In this case the ravens are nothing but phantoms, animated phantoms directly from

the house with red lights, the daylight reddens early in winter,

(Coughing)

excuse me, I have something in my throat, it feels scratchy,

like having a wire filament in my throat,

and as far as the ravens go,

(Coughing)

but you know, I don't have to say anything

there's something scratchy in my throat. My skin is becoming thinner, I know without having to check that it's probably glowing, there are beads of sweat on my forehead again, but hopefully no one will be coming round with full glasses, and no one will say cheers.

9

Seeing and Hearing

LAST SUMMER I HAD THE CHANCE to book an inexpensive hour-long flight in a private airplane. The pilot was said to be an actor, but an experienced and enthusiastic pilot nonetheless. Upon learning that he had built his own plane, I was so astonished that I kept asking more and more questions. Soon I found myself negotiating a private flight, and I thought I could no longer back out.

Two or three days later I was standing on an airfield south of the river Thur and waiting; it turned out that I had driven to an airfield that was only for glider planes. Someone on the large, green field pointed me to the right airfield on a map. I got there late, but the field was empty. A few women and men were sitting with drinks in a nondescript wooden hut on the edge of the concrete strip. They said that a red airplane had just been in contact and would definitely be there soon. They also told me how much an hour-long flight with them would cost, and it was roughly the same amount I had arranged to pay for my inexpensive flight. Some time later, a plane circled in the sky above me, and there was something very direct about the way it landed, as if a car was driving straight at me.

Then the actor climbed out of the plane and approached me on foot, and I went out to the airfield with him and climbed on board. I had to take off the hat I'd brought as a precaution and received a pair of headphones in return, because he said that although it was a small plane, you couldn't hear a word without headphones. It's strange to think that the official aerial pose, the official sky and air pose, starts with headphones. Like two air force officers wearing black earmuffs, able to see each other's faces only in profile, we started trundling a few meters along the bumpy ground, and the moment of liftoff was unmistakable, as if we were driving except in three dimensions. While we strained to climb higher and higher, as if we were climbing a steep hill, the pilot told me that he had built the plane himself, and I was no longer surprised by this fact. He said he preferred having the wings above the body of the plane rather than below it, because it made for a better view. I easily recognized the streets I knew, the bridges, highways, woods, where the railway tracks led, and no part of the view was obstructed by wings fitted in the wrong place. These technical questions aside, it was a good day for flying, and there was no fog or rain. The Thur lay beneath us, and instead of appearing to flow, it was rigid like plaster and bottle-green. Underground the Thur is the biggest river in Europe, and if you know that fact you can see it that way, whereas someone who doesn't know that won't get much out of the aerial view, since you can't see what's underground.

Whenever the pilot explained something, I could hear nothing but crackling. I must be height-deaf, I thought.

After a few exchanges, he realized that I couldn't hear his questions because my headphones hadn't been set up correctly, but since they couldn't be fixed midflight, I would remain partly deaf for the rest of the flight.

We had agreed that he would fly at a height of only five or six hundred meters. The pilot said that in populated areas that was not allowed, but outside those areas he would fly lower as I had requested, and when we had left the last village behind us, we dropped to half the height we were flying at, to the height we had agreed upon. The hills beneath us were nearly flat, rolled flat, scraped flat, barely worth calling hills, although they divided the Untersee or western tip of Lake Constance from the Thur region; I could only recognize the features of the ancient mountains by picking out buildings along the roads and in the woods.

Then we flew across the woods, and in a clearing of sorts I saw a little affair, entwined bodies twisting on a blue blanket, two bodies. We could easily make out people on the ground, which meant that down below you didn't only have to worry about being disturbed by someone coming from the side or behind, but also from the air, as in wartime. Regardless of whether you were lying on the ground, running, or just standing there, a red gnat like this one might be following you, and every person, road, and farmhouse could be in peril.

After flying over the hilly plains we found ourselves above Lake Constance, the Rhine flowing closely along the lake's southern banks while barely intermingling with its waters, and on the northern side the town of Meersburg and one village after another.

I hadn't planned to fly over the lake, but we spent at least ten minutes hovering above the water with its white lines, its lighter and darker patches. The surface of the lake looked rigid, just as the Thur had, the waves stood still, and the different colors did not move. We roared over the marvelously colored sheets of lake toward Bregenz, which looked just the way it does on a map. Everything looked like a map. What was I doing flying over maps? I was sitting in a plane that was not inexpensive and flying over maps.

The man next to me pointed upward at a few other airplanes, sideways at a flock of birds that had just swooped beneath us, and showed me several helicopters, kites circling, white gulls further below, and between us and the other planes, two propeller-driven planes. You should look at the sky, he said after we had landed. He had already tried to explain this to me when we were in the air, while I was preoccupied with our agreed-upon height of five to six hundred meters, with wanting to see the overgrown old walls and paths that had sunk into the ground. I had read that they could be seen from this height, without stopping to think about the fact that you had to be able to recognize what you wanted to see, otherwise you might think you were looking at an arid field down below because you noticed a light-colored patch, without realizing that it was actually the remains of a Roman settlement, or think that a Roman settlement was hidden in the light-colored ground, when it was nothing but a dry field.

I know that the earth in these parts, the topsoil at least, is dark brown, nearly umber. The ground could just as easily be yellow, copper red or black, and the fields could be strewn with stones, but they aren't. In some aerial pictures you can see pale rectangular shapes and straight lines. The remains of Roman walls probably lie hidden in plain sight, as it were, the rectangles are buried farmhouses, and the long lines indicate where the streets used to run. I used to know that and still do, but I don't know anything else, maybe I've been sitting in an airplane forever and am still in one, and meanwhile the headphones have been fixed.

10

Tarzan

IN THE MORNINGS no one would be out and about up in Hohenhart, not at 10 on a Sunday. I. wouldn't have to talk to anyone or do voice tests on a Sunday morning, she wouldn't have to think about whether her pronunciation was acceptable, whether a deeper or a higher-pitched voice would sound better, and whether or not dogs had to be spoken to in an especially high-pitched voice. High C or a few notes higher would probably be about right for enticing small children or dogs. She was bowlegged. She walked straight ahead with her dog, went up the hill, and then walked a few hundred meters toward the village of about ten houses below. As she walked, it occurred to her that she and her dog could, in a sense, break into this peaceful village, that's what it would look like. *There goes a stranger, she's too tall, there she goes speaking indistinctly or all too distinctly in that deep voice of hers, which doesn't change at all even when she's calling to that small dog,* I. thought, but the little one still came to her wagging its tail. When they arrived at the first house, a cat looked at them, it was lying comfortably across the door, indifferent to passersby since it was protected from the back, behind it two dogs were barking, one of which stayed out of sight, whereas the other poked its skull through the

cat flap, about to burst through the flap and jump out, as if
the cat flap were a trap door in the *Rosenkavalier*, although
the *Rosenkavalier* wouldn't mean anything here, in fact it
would mean nothing at all. To explain that story you would
need twenty trap doors to fly open at once, all revealing
children's heads, their mouths open, calling for the same
papa, whereas here only the dog in the kennel was snarling
and barking, and she and her little dog were hurrying on,
both keeping quiet so as not to have to submit to a voice
test, having figured out that they would get through most
easily that way, the only disadvantage being that they had
already somewhat lost their voices, they went a few steps
further, turned right, wanted to go up the path back to the
car, that was the route they had planned, but there was a
big blond curly-haired dog standing in their way, or rather,
coming toward them incredibly slowly and decisively. She
had already run into this massive dog once, that time it had
approached her, not in an unfriendly manner, but a man
had whistled it back and kicked it, actually kicked it hard
in the side and the head, and sent it back through the door
into a deep dark house or a barn. I. had thought at the time
that kicking a dog like that would certainly change the animal, and it did. The dog stood in the path and barked with
its head lowered, as if it had been replaced by a different
dog, there was no time to think, she called out to it in her
ordinary speaking voice, telling it not to move, and hastened
along with her little dog, not up the path toward the car,
but down the hill to a huge deserted meadow further along,
she paced up and down but couldn't think what to do, and
eventually she tied her dog to a tree, the dog sat hesitantly

even though it didn't know why it was sitting there, and she climbed the path alone, wondering how she would make it to the car and then back down to the tree. Anyway, she thought, dogs usually have it in for other dogs, not for people, and if it was still standing there, she would try a higher-pitched voice, *yes come right over here you little Hündeli* she would say in Swiss German, although she hadn't yet found the right pitch in her throat. When she went a little further up the slope, the dog was still standing in the corner where she had left it, there wasn't any way around it, and it seemed complacently enraged when she reappeared. Then she saw a tractor from the farm driving toward the yard, again there wasn't time to think, she started waving to the driver, who waved back almost instantly, except there was trouble bubbling, something had gone wild, had lost its head, was headless, was getting out of control, and she tried to scatter her fears, but they fluttered about like dandelion heads, though it was long past the season for dandelions and they had a different name here in Switzerland. A thin man sat on the tractor—he had switched off the motor—in short frayed trousers and a gray shirt, he was getting out of the seat and coming toward her, it would make for a good Sunday afternoon. *Hoi*, he called out and was happy. She herself attempted a pale generic smile, turned to the man in high spirits, high-pitched and pale, and asked whether the dog on the road would bite. The man didn't understand her and said *Hoi* again, and she thought, *beißen* is a good word because it's clear, *biesse* also means bite and might have been a good choice, even better in this case, someone would have to quickly decide which version was more correct, in Middle

High German *biesse* would have been correct, but to make yourself understood you would have to say *beißen*, and the matter at hand was the blond dog's unambiguous intention to *beißen*, a matter of actual or threatened biting, although to be sure you could also go crazy wondering why a certain person didn't understand a certain word. Flies, wasps, and butterflies hovered about them. The man told her to sit down first. He said he also needed to get his bearings. He happily began a long speech in which every word smelled like schnapps, he said she would have to stay there, that his name was *Tarzan*, or that the dog's name was *Tarzan*, that it was an alert, hardworking animal; the mailman or *Pöstler* comes every day with a *Guetsli* or cookie to mollify the dog, he said raptly, while the sun shined and there was no one about for miles. She was momentarily happy to have understood a few words despite his speaking in dialect, and she quickly took a dog biscuit from her coat pocket, while the man slapped his legs, his schnapps-impaired legs, he had the advantage of being in a familiar place, and her insinuation that his dog was in some way suspect had given meaning to his Sunday, and besides, he was also surprised to have understood what she was saying, so he kept talking, gradually becoming jollier, he spoke forcefully to his dog, which was now nestling up against her legs, lo and behold, while her own dog was still waiting down in the meadow, it probably couldn't hear a thing from that distance. The increasingly happy man said he was about to light his own house or the tractor on fire, but then he decided to open the door, and she had to enter the barn right away, the curly-haired dog barking behind her, while close behind the dog came the man.

11

Anyhowever

THE TERMINATION LETTER came in mid-November; four employees in my department would have to be terminated as part of a downsizing plan, the letter said, and I tried not to think too hard about it, because I had just had pneumonia and was supposed to rest as much as possible, which meant I was under instructions to recuperate, avoid work, and avoid brooding over things.

Lying in bed with my legs elevated, I was ready to clear my mind when a song came into my head, and I sang it for about half an hour until a second song occurred to me, after which another and yet another song were lying in wait, descending into my head like airplanes descending into busy airports from who knows where, in a visible row, landing one after another, *Bonny and Clyde, they lived a lot together, Baker man is bakin' bread, The night train is comin', Amor, amor, amor, this little word tells you that I love you.* The offensive lasted all day, and a week later I had found no other way of dealing with it but to write down the titles or the opening lines of the songs, after two weeks I had three hundred titles on my list, so that I had to arrange them alphabetically just to have a good grasp of them all, but there was still no end in sight to the music in my head.

Saying they landed in my head may not be the best way
of putting it, it felt more like they were sliding to the front
of my mind from an overlooked storeroom somewhere in
the back, and I couldn't just replace them there, I had to
deal with them as they came, look at them, sing through
them, *Ich will keine Schokolade, ich will lieber einen Mann*,
My baby just cares for me, *What do you get if you fall in love*. I
could only silence one song by proceeding to the next one.
Or rather, the songs mostly came in twos and even threes, I
don't know how they were organized, in fact, I'd be curious
to know how and why certain songs went together. Many
seemed to have been stored together according to the particular words they contained, after *Pineapples, come buy my
pineapples*, came *Choco, choco, chocolate, oh Signore please,
buy your wife some choco, choco* . . . and then came the banana
songs, other fruits, and right after that "Griechischer Wein,"
and because Greece is inseparable from the sea, all the songs
that had something to do with seas or oceans came next,
like "Sixteen Tons," *Some people say a man is made outta
mud*. There's a German version of that song, about a boy
who becomes a sailor at fourteen, the song sounds better in
English but I like it even in translation, and apart from that
only the most dreadful hit songs came to mind.

Every now and then, when I sat down at the table and
began to reflect on some concrete matter, the songs would
recede and I would begin to fret about how I lost my job
and needed to find a new job, I thought about which com-
panies weren't firing people and where I could get hired, and
I began to make phone calls. I made some progress and got a
few good leads, but whenever my call was being transferred I

would hear music on the other end of the line, and when the music stopped I would listen to the HR people's explanations, promises, and slight evasions, and then I would think about the kind of job I really needed, what I really needed. *All you need is love, pa pa rapapam*, was what came to mind, because music was always lurking in the background, even when I was supposedly thinking about something else, I'll have to describe this to a neurologist, there was always a subliminal level of noise in my head, constant musical programming, *Sailing down my golden river, These boots are made for walking, Hang down your head, Tom Dooley, poor boy, you're bound to die, I shot the Sheriff, Ohh summer wine.* The ad industry has long been aware of this mechanism, they know you can sink into music as if it were a bog, and regardless of what they're selling, all that matters is that the jingles stick, and stick they do, in fact other people figured this out long before the ad execs did, or there wouldn't be so many marches whose whole point is to flip a switch in the brain that makes people better at marching.

As I was lying in bed with more than four hundred song titles around me, I was going crazy wondering why the worse hits surfaced before the better ones, given that I was still preoccupied with vocal music, since I naturally couldn't have incorporated instrumental music into my alphabetical list, and somehow no instrumental pieces came to mind because I had no plans to incorporate them, which is also strange, so it was only after I had collected more than four hundred titles that I noticed how many songs had to do with the names of women, or even began with women's names, they must all have been belated *Minnelieder. Hello Mary*

Lou, good-bye heart, Hey Mrs. Robinson, Matilda, she take me money, I'll paint you a picture, Cindy Lou, Marina, Marina. I think there are fewer lyrics like this now, maybe we're taking a break from *Minnesang*, glimpses into love stories involving Juanita or Anita are out of fashion, but stories never go out of fashion, stories told in two or three words, only now the words have barbs that sink into your head, somewhere in the back of your head, they clamp on, crowding in, waiting for a brief moment of weakness, a moment of instability, to erupt one after another and overrun all your thinking.

After five weeks there was a murmur in my head, *anyhowever, anyhowever,* it was barely even intelligible, there's a song that goes like that, there must be. After six weeks, my list had 732 entries, which is interesting if only because I have been told that many people manage with a vocabulary of about a thousand words in their native language, in which case there would be roughly the same number of songs as words, even if the effect is not comparable. The lyrical offensive is anything but restful, it certainly isn't helping me get better. Meanwhile I have become less sure of myself even when making phone calls, and as soon as my head begins to ring with noise I say: Wrong number! Wrong number! and hang up. I hardly see anyone anymore, I wouldn't know what to talk about. In the evenings I laugh to myself and solve crossword puzzles all night long, all night long, god of love, four letters, *Amor, Amor, Amo-o-or!*

12

Pierre

It's just us two down by the lake, the two of us, we're stand-ing there, walking east along the row of white houses by the lakefront, we turn back and end up sitting in a café, in the present—at the lakefront everything is present tense—before going further up the hill in Lausanne. Here down below in Ouchy it's the present tense as we agreed, we, we're drinking our first glass of wine, *we are drinking*, further up is the future, *we will drink*, and even further up is further than the future, a subjunctive, which expresses a type of possibility, and can be found at the highest point of the city, a conditional, *we would drink*, we would like to do that, and so we do. Our hotel is up there, the wine is down by the lake, and Pierre says, don't forget we only have three days, that too is a question of time.

Down here at the lake the wind is blowing from Geneva, there are three people coming toward us, then a group of four, then just two, a young couple who are probably from around here, the man with black hair looks at her mouth while he speaks, she has a mound of short red curls, and her opinions match her looks.

Pierre is saying something to me in a purr, which is to say that his voice sinks deep into his throat in the manner typical of Romance languages and these well-oiled Romanic throats! We should head back up, he says, and we will, we would climb, will have climbed, once we had begun our climb, would be correct. The young couple walks ahead of us. The girl is limping a little but if it hurts she's trying not to let it show. First the two of them walk up, then us, then four more people behind us, that's what cities are like, we're climbing into the future, or rather the city is climbing. It's eleven in the morning, the city is in its April winter, even here it's not always (always is also a time) as far south as you might think, every hundred years or so the winter breaks into Lausanne, sometimes more often than that, and in the streets lie piles of unexpected snow.

Earlier this month there was a fire in a nearby detention center for asylum seekers, says the news on the radio, and there's also an unsettling report of a landslide at a construction site in the city center, which represents the city's substratum.

Each person has at least one amoeba that keeps contorting and distorting itself, making its host hot, cold, and sometimes sick.

We say *we* to distinguish ourselves from the city's tourists, who wouldn't say *we*, or at least not *we tourists*, that's for others to say about them, and the label never quite seems to fit, because you could say that practically the whole world is populated by tourists, a certain percentage of the world's population, perhaps a tenth, periodically moves somewhere in order to be tourists. The Japanese come to Lausanne and take the old subway, the M2, down to the waterfront promenade, we are told, yet we don't see any Japanese tourists and hear plenty of Spanish instead. There are South American and lately Russian tourists going up and down, that's the first distinction we learn to make, and next we learn to distinguish sport tourists from cultural tourists. In Lausanne the latter crowd around the cathedral. Cathedral-cultural tourists also look different from museum tourists. While traveling they refer to themselves as *we* or *us* when they're talking to fellow travelers, *there are thirty of us* or something like that, but they don't say *we tourists, we're dragging our small new suitcases through the steep city*, it's always they, the city is full of tourists dragging their suitcases through the city, taking the M2 to Ouchy and up into the center, to Flon, and although we're told that no Lausanner rides the funicular called the Strick, we spot them on it anyway, with their strollers and shopping bags.

At eleven we start doing inner gymnastics in the steep city. We have arranged to meet at a restaurant down by the lake. I am sitting at a large wooden table, across the street from the glass-walled facade of a castle which is also a restaurant. These glass-encased facades with wooden strutting between panes of glass are a dream, I am sitting outside, they set the table quickly, the sun crept up an hour ago, there's snow up there and April warmth down here, the bare, gnarled plane trees. And as Pierre appears from among the wandering crowds, I recognize him right away, within seconds, I recognize him almost before I can see him, that's what it's always been like.

As if his were the only possible male form, and no other thinner, fatter, taller, shorter, darker, blonder, nor any other male form was possible, all other forms are superfluous.

From down there it's a vertical climb, we follow the Metro line on foot, upward, into the future. Although I have forever been repeating: there's nothing but the Now. Who needs the past and the other tenses, I repeat, and I say *good afternoon*, there's nothing but now.

Pierre adds up the past and drinks a glass of wine, steeling himself not to make a long face. The past is beautiful, he says, and falls right into it. That past belongs to us. He plunges into it, but it won't always have him because it is past, and I can barely haul him out, or he me. But since the past in Lausanne lies in the lake (that's a conjecture, I don't know for sure since there haven't been many excavations), it's wet and gets in your eyes, on the other hand, the eyes— those *Augen*—can also remind you of the past.

As I was driving to Lausanne, the German around me gradually dissolved, first the sign *Jardin* appeared next to *Saatgut* and many German words, and then more and more French appeared. Are the languages at each other's throats or in each other's arms, or have they mistaken each other for themselves? Biel is like this too. Bilingual. Split tongues.

Gradually even the graffiti becomes French. But then a large sign appears in English: *Garden*. And: *Do It Yourself.* That is suggestive. (What should you do yourself? Speak French, even if you can't really?)

From Bern onwards we find the April snow that was announced on the radio, even before we reach Grandvaux, the French-speaking hills full of vineyards.

The two languages are eating each other up, they're in each other's mouths, and from Romont onward it's clear that French is doing the devouring, German has almost disappeared in the mouth of French, which makes this indisputably a love story.

And because this is about Lausanne, I am thinking not in German but in a Romance language, French, of course, no one notices, but I'm basically speaking French here, which requires swapping out my thinking and not just my words.

The hotel is further up, almost as far as the cathedral, and later I will be able to say we slept up there, which constitutes an augmentation even though it's in the past. Just now, as though I were to say, sleepabanaban. Sleepabanabanaban, now that sounds more like Spanish than French, but it has to be a form you can imagine, in which the longer ago something happened, the more syllables must be tacked onto the word, that's something you can prove. It was a while back. Sleep, and years later, sleepabanabanaban. The future is sleeparanara, which sounds like a Romance language to both of us. Lausanners are good with tenses and can stuff them into a single word, as opposed to grappling with dubious compounds that crumble into blurry wills and woulds.

They leap up and down between buildings with crisp words.

After breakfast we read the paper in Café Grutier, beneath the hotel, and in an hour they played *All that she wants is another baby* three times in a row, in the next place we go to they're playing *Memories are made of this*, there had to be music pouring over your head, the lyrics were only an afterthought, we got to an electronics shop where we bought batteries, a young salesperson was bounding about, a skinny guy who seemed to be neither adult nor child, he'll always stay that way, nice, skinny, he'll never grow up, he leaped around the shop to the sound of an Italian song and sang along with it while he was ringing us up, not that it was even a nice song, it was a jilted lover singing cheerfully about his loneliness as if it were a good thing, as if there were a rule stipulating that everything you long for absolutely always without exception has to vanish. *You want another baby* and we're out.

We're above it all, that's what we've got, being above things.

At the port we're standing in our own present. Walking along together, just us two, going a few meters higher, sitting down and drinking, the pronoun *we* marks an augmentation from the singular to the plural, without even having to change tenses. We seem to have found yet another bar where at least half the patrons are tourists, visitors to Lausanne. Pierre likes that. He looks across the Alps to the south, which is where his sunny face comes from, his serious sunny face, a mouth which can be and is silent, which has a friendly way of speaking. While he is thinking, he lowers his heavy southern face so he can think, and because we exchanged a couple of words with the people sitting at the next table, he buys them a coffee.

Until we have every word in our grasp, he says. Every word, what is meant by it, what it intends and what it can say. Every word, yeah right.

When I drink a coffee alone, saying *I drink* sounds better than using the impersonal gerund, *drinking*. I would rather say *I sit* than talk about *sitting, drinking, walking*. Further uphill, sitting together represents another augmentation, we will have a drink, you have to imagine that in a Romance language, *nous buvons*, *boirons*, and at the top lies the subjunctive, the tense of possibility. We would sit. We would, that's further up, further along than what's happening right this moment.

The six of us talk. Pierre has been chatting with the people at the next table, two older and two younger men, fathers and sons, all from Lausanne, they say, I'm sitting in a fog of words, unable to understand all the words they're using, and one of the fathers asks why there aren't any ideal men, images, ideal images. Why aren't there! Pierre looks at him slowly, narrows his eyes, or rather lowers his eyelids, in order to see more clearly, he has pirate eyes, and slowly asks if not having ideals is a custom, either a new or an old custom, what's a custom anyway, he adds. Instead of answering him, the others nod. Pierre's French sounds Spanish, and the four of them think about what their question might have to do with customs, maybe it was a misunderstanding, they say, and I look over their heads, so that no one will think my ideal consists with one of the present company.

Think about what happens to you when you have to speak a foreign language, Pierre says. It's tragic! It's happening to me now, because I'm speaking French and have to hold back four-fifths of my thoughts, Pierre says.

A black woman with a leather cap on her head is sitting at the next table. She smiles over at me and we come to an understanding, while the others are preoccupied with their dreams, and Pierre treats the four of them to a glass of wine.

Even in Lausanne, nearly every person is translated. It's true that in all the streets and bars they speak original

French, which is not what I mean, nor do I think that more people are translated here than in other places, what I actually mean is that Pierre is not a translation, he is the opposite of a translation.

About halfway up, just above Flon, Lausanne becomes a construction site, this is where the future is constructed, it's been like this since forever, which is to say that the future has never been within reach.

I, for one, am ruling the future out anyway, whereas Pierre dreams of it every now and then and tells me about his dreams, even though I don't like that word, because dreams aren't the same thing as plans, what's a dream supposed to mean anyway, I say, but he waves his hand dismissively, he's sure I'm mixing up the words.

We ascend. By Avenue de la Gare we are halfway up, in the conditional. Down by the lake is our past, part of which is anything but cheerful, but all this time we have loved the melancholy.

Further up the hill, by definition, is the peak, the hotel, at the bottom of the lake is the past, the past perfect, there Pierre lies with his gray-green pirate eyes and ever so slightly furrowed brow, exactly how he looked when he first peered into where we are standing now, into the future, and there on the lakebed he lies with his honest hands and even his honest gait, not that he can walk while he is lying on the lakebed, but that was back then, and it would be wrong to claim that what used to be the case no longer exists: right now our most pressing question is what to do with the past.

At half past eight in the evening it is still bright outside, but indoors the lights are already on, and an hour later the lights will be flickering in the distance by the southern shore. At night the great lake becomes a black hole, but we've gone over that already.

We're water polo players, I say the next day. With our heads, shoulders, and arms visible above water, anyone can see all our movements, we've got it all under control, but under the surface we're treading water, our stomachs and most of our spines and hearts are underwater, above water we're clearly visible, but everything below the collarbone is private.

As I've said, I don't want to know much about the past, or at least up until now I didn't, the Now is enough, it's enough for now, is what I've said all this time, but it's gradually starting to not be true, and as if I wanted to catch up on a past I would otherwise shake off, and even to take on other people's pasts, I pounce on words that are somewhat older than I am. Pierre is like that too, there are certain words he's crazy about, *vuelve loco por algunas palabras.* Years ago he came into my bookstore, not that he ever came to the bookstore again, but that time he bought four different dictionaries and a grammar book.

In Lausanne he shows me Spanish words, the *here* and *there* alone, just imagine that, he says, *aquí y allí*, he motions to the street with his hand to demonstrate, and he also shows me how he cannot escape his own *here*, cannot forge past it, everywhere is *here*, wherever he's standing is *here*, and those two words describe more than just the landscape. Ascending and descending, as he does, suits this place. Only in Lausanne is French called for, tongues have always moved this way here, here (here!) local tongues grow either larger or broader, and they taste of old words that other people have already had on their tongues, I would rather not picture that in detail, so many strange tongues with their private affairs, I have to repress the mental image, and up on the Grand Pont, which looks like the kind of bridge someone must have jumped off at some point, not that I asked, but it does look as though you could throw yourself off it when in a dangerous mood, almost as though the immense height had been created specifically so people could jump off it, up there on the bridge, because your mouth goes dry up there. The words change, Pierre says. Up there different words occur to you, and there's so much air in your lungs.

As soon as I'm no longer in Lausanne, I begin to think that the city is so steep that you could throw yourself into the lake from the cathedral, but you couldn't do that, there would be no audience from the lake, you'd have to be jumping for yourself, and neither the lonely mountains over there in France, which you can see from here, nor the lake itself would be watching.

But why kill yourself? Every now and again we travel somewhere together, every few weeks or months, of course there's all the time in between, but we're above all that.

In the meantime he's nearly gouged one of his eyes out, nearly lopped off a hand, he could have sawed his leg off, or kept quiet for ten days, once his head threatened to burst on him, and again he just kept quiet, then he grew fatter, as he tells it, which actually sort of suited him, then he was treated badly for a while, and he kept quiet, as he always did when provoked, but he had recovered by the time he came to Lausanne.

Winter's not letting up, the ravens starve and fall dead onto the roads. Love itself has frozen, people just stare at posters, everyone's out of town and all plans are on ice. Rather, it's so cold that people start getting cozy. They crawl into themselves and refuse to see anyone, they wear hoods and have tears in their eyes. Because it's so cold, they bounce up and down and stretch as though they're warming up, even though they speak French, and lust and love have been hidden in sport, even in the cold.

Global warming sounds beautiful. Everyone wants warmth and intimacy at all costs, and what more could one want than global warming. But there are ravens falling, starved, from the sky. (The ravens are my sons, I say. Our sons. Why not daughters, asks Pierre. Because that would make him a fairy-tale stepfather, I say, which he isn't.)

In the morning a raven falls into the lake before my eyes, into the Lac Léman, straight into its own past.

Pierre shakes his head. Let's leave the sky to the angels and the sparrows, he says, and then sparrows are falling from the sky too, the blackbirds hurtling after them, heavy as lead, no longer hungry, just apathetic, one more blackbird falls, it plunges, and I fall with it.

And everyone is intoxicated, drunk, life is intoxication, you're trying to keep your head above it, your head juts out of the fog like a mountain peak seen from a plane, and it tries to think straight, though soberness itself usually ends up being intoxicating, and there's also a certain ascetic intoxication, it doesn't help to be alone, nor does it help to be wading through the intoxication with someone else.

How long this all takes! The past perfect, and before it the Ice Age. Back then I was really in love, love isn't even the right word for it, we could have permitted ourselves other words, I looked through the lake into the future, and I was so short of breath that it hurt.

But can verbs lie? Are they the liars? Maybe they are, many of them are hiding and saying *I'll see* or *I would*—and this *would* is, in the end, fundamentally dishonest.

There are night verbs and day verbs too, among them minor scales, and somewhere behind them is the ideal image.

Back then I was still lying down below, in all likelihood there was no lake as yet, in any case I was sure, I was pretty well sure of myself, and saw all the good things that lay ahead of me, the future, an endless good future lay ahead of me, and it nearly tore my chest open, even if you were perfectly happy, that would be a cross to bear.

This morning we are climbing into the lake's past. I saw him, I had seen him, and we looked out toward Geneva with our eyes closed.

Today at eleven in the morning we look out onto the vacant lake. No ships. One big red workboat, then no other sign of movement all morning.

At first, in Ouchy, a classical white catches the eye, soothing facades, beautifully formed balconies with their protrusions and indentations, a soothing white lakefront consisting of houses, urban soothing facilitated by houses, just the way Lucerne or Montreux have it, if you look harder you can pick out individual colors, pink, light turquoise, yellow, lots of southern yellows and blues, Pierre says the bright yellow is his favorite, and just as the mountains all look the same at first glance, the houses along the promenade all look the same until gradually you can make out individual houses, balconies, sun umbrellas, and awnings.

At eleven the following morning it begins to rain, colorful umbrellas appear next to colorful blinds, and beneath them the guttural and trilled sounds continue to purr, meeting in all the different r's there are. The guttural r and the trilled r look each other in the eye like two different species challenging one another to a fight, or maybe they just want someone to look them in the mouth. I don't look just anyone in the mouth, says Pierre.

We are researchers, we're experimenting, we take risks. We try things, and sometimes things crash.

We take what the metro calls the Blue Line to Flon, to the foot of the huge gray bridge, even the gray of the bridge is a huge gray, and near the pillars and further up on the pedestrian level there's always construction, mountain goats used to leap up and down here, this you can tell by looking at the passersby, the future of the mountain goats, who can catch their breath once they get to Flon. The Romans built the higher parts of the city as a strategic move, a defensive one, of course, and the cathedral was built later, also as a strategic move.

It's 5:20 on an April morning, with no day in sight. We close our eyes for a few minutes, waiting for daylight, until we're convinced that it's morning, I love the morning. Next door, behind the wall, there's multi-layered snoring.

We sleep in the highest hotel, and in the morning we can look out across the city toward the lake. There is no tense higher than *I would have had*, where could you go from there, *we would have had* is already so much.

The hotel is about as old as the big museum below. The house opposite us was painted green and also built in a classical style, somewhat further down the slope and several meters lower than the hotel, the house behind it is even lower, and each subsequent house is lower still. Our hotel is mostly occupied by single women with clever, independent faces who open the doors to their rooms and sit in the lobby.

At breakfast, Pierre said he's always joking, he only ever jokes, and he leaves the table with an uncertain or thoughtful gait, to bring me bread and ham. Unfortunately there is no white toast.

I never tell jokes, he says at breakfast on the second day, and as he is leaving the table to get buns and butter, he looks like he's going to think about something on the way or is about to remember something.

He has been thinking about times again, and finally about departure times, his face gets longer and longer, he gets another mug of coffee, stares into the mug, and says, yesterday, tomorrow, in a sense it's all the same to him, and he rambles on about how he can't distinguish between days and wouldn't ever want to anyway. If he isn't allowed to imagine yesterday and tomorrow and all the other times at once, then he doesn't need them at all. He draws his good broad hand from the tablecloth, the hand disappears, and he looks around, so you can tell he isn't seeing anything right now. Longing into the past is a joke, like running against the wind. That's a nice way of putting it, I say. He doesn't like my saying that, what's the point of saying that, and that's the end of the conversation.

Not long ago he said he'd cried over a sentence, and now he is claiming he would never cry, on the other hand, he would never say he'd never cry, he gets up and walks carefully toward the front desk, and I have known for a while that he isn't making any assertions, he wants something that lies between his *here* and his *over there* (Figaro qua, Figaro là), and in German this in-between place might be called *da*, there. Being there, no jokes, no crying, no time. Language doesn't lend itself to putting things more precisely, who could say this more precisely.

For instance, there's the collective will out there on campus, where students are always coming one by one out of the sprawling buildings and stepping onto the sprawling lawns, the newly liberated students with their cluttered, dazzled heads walking through the park without looking left or right, they get on bicycles or into cars, but most of them wander, saunter, or stride to the M1 Metro station, preoccupied, sunk in embraces, and take the train bound for Flon into the city, where this is the last stop, everyone please leave the train, and before they get there, even before they leave for there or for somewhere else, they can't possibly know what they will be thinking in twenty years, nor can they possibly care, they walk to the station arm-in-arm and with a freedom in their necks, the freedom is less visible in their gait than in their necks, and although later they will know or at least be able to find out what they thought then of the lawns, the embraces, the full heads, and the buildings, they don't yet know how it will later strike them, although they might think they do.

Madame, Hemingway said, not that these were his exact words, sometimes it happens that a bull falls in love with a cow and ignores the other cows. The story inevitably has a fatal ending, at the very latest when they both die.

The perpetual motion of small suitcases through the city center, some of which have bombs in them, one explodes in the middle of the street, the future collapses, everything you believed in is over, a landslide.

My peace is gone, my heart is sore, a student said after the explosion. She was quoting Goethe.

Nearly everything is translation, unfortunately, the original would have been the ideal, who wouldn't rather have the original, the non-translation is what people want.

Pierre said on the phone a few days ago that worries only multiply. Worries multiply, and of course we can defend ourselves, but not like pachyderms. We are always talking about pachyderms, as though we had huge warm intimate interiors, but it is the other way around, we are smooth on the outside and hard on the inside. Fruit on the outside, like a ripe apricot, and stone hard on the inside.

We once talked (at night, in the middle of the night with a bottle of wine) about all the contrary, contradictory, incompatible, meaningless, unrealistic things people have expected of each other since at least the Ice Age, all the intense expectations people harbor in vain, since all expectations are harbored in vain, and every time someone's expectations are partially fulfilled, which is possible, at least that's what we've always tried to emphasize, that such a thing is possible, so then when it happens, which is simply inconceivable, especially for the person who has those expectations, it means a saeculum has passed.

All the way from the station to Flon, up sixty-seven steps and a steep street without steps. This is a neighborhood made for your calves. In this neighborhood, which is tiring for the calves, we add up the present, in a flat, comfortable landscape, we could also say that the present is here with me, that the future is further away, and a further future is even further away, a future reality, one person could call this future a dream, another could call it a plan, and a third person could call it a possibility (the subjunctive), anyone could spread the past out in a flat landscape, but these things are easier to imagine in Lausanne, except for the fact that you feel the elevation in your calves.

In Biel it all merges together, plains, hills, German, French, street names, affection, aversion, and all their augmented, superlative forms.

Lord Byron spent the summer of 1816 living down by the lake in a hotel-restaurant with an English name, and while lodging there he wrote a whole book (a plaque by the entrance tells you which one). These days they play Italian music in the restaurant, the coffee is served with biscotti, *cantucci alle mandorle*, earlier at lunch at Le Ticino a Portuguese waiter served us. That was a significant meeting of Romance languages and songs in Lausanne. Maybe I will be able to write songs myself someday! Three hundred and sixty, eight hundred or six hundred and sixty-six songs for the visitor to Lausanne, for the battered pirate who looks about in the lake air, for his steady gaze, his sideways glance. Songs about the gaze and the eyes and songs for the pirate, who harbors his memories for years. I don't know how he does it, how he keeps it up, maybe by looking around in a certain way.

And what you can love out of someone is hard to grasp, we had already talked about that, loving the peace or the laughter out of someone, for instance, even if the phrase doesn't sound right.

Pierre can arrange spaces in his head and then stow them away as though they had never been there, keep on talking, and at some point retrieve something he's stowed away, as though it were not a memory but fresh as dew, as if he can see it immediately in front of him.

At the tall gray bridge Pierre loses his calm, and I see the mountain goats from an earlier time leap up and down the steep paths with their half-frightened confident faces, while the people eat and drink on the street in French, *takeaway, ils boivent, ils mangent.* At the only stationery shop we finally found, Pierre bought pens and notebooks, but he said we shouldn't write down everything that concerned the two of us, and in the bookstore, there aren't many bookstores left in Lausanne either, he looked for textbooks about Arabic, Indian, and Chinese script.

Steep city. Sunday, eleven, Café Grutier. Once in a century.

If anything, I know his balance wheel well, it's the kind clocks have, old-fashioned analog clocks, one of those tiny mechanical components that would hold a clock's movement in a calibrated imbalance, that held and hold it to its own tempo. Digital clocks probably don't have such mechanical components.

It has stopped raining, the lake is as gray as it was before, a southern Alpine lake in an unimaginable gray, populated by a single red ship, that's how we'll enter it in the books.

Then I sit here on a bench, alone, waiting, later I will sit of my own free will at a table at the back of the Restaurant du Port, waiting, I have a little smoke alarm inside me (instead of a weather station), a smoke alarm that describes not only the quantity but also the direction of my inner smoke, and I notice it flickering like fire and changing every instant. In all seriousness, what I claimed to think a few minutes ago no longer holds true, likewise desires blur, outside it is raining again, I sit at the furthest table in the back, without sobbing, without crying, and my tears flow wordlessly, soundlessly, so I drink a hot chocolate and the rain sobs from the Bois de Sauvabelin, from Montbenon, the Rue Madeleine, the Rue du Petit-Chêne, the Rue de la Grotte, the Avenue d'Ouchy, and from yet other streets all the way down to the lake and reaches it, and it takes a while for all the available water to trickle out of you without a sob, as it just flows out from your eyes.

Folded into the cloth napkin lying on the unused plate before me is a metro ticket. Like a piece of hair. A metro ticket could be a piece of hair if it's stuck to a napkin. These disgusting intimacies.

An Englishman is sitting at the next table. His idea of the future is vaguer than anyone else's in the city. He believes that the future is dependent upon his own will. He wants to leave by train tomorrow, he will, that's what he'll do. And in fact the man will probably get his way and actually leave. We'll also be leaving tomorrow, but that is independent of our will.

We, and here I have to at least mention that Pierre's name is not Pierre even if that's what we're calling him (we couldn't call him Eduard), but how can this go on when I keep getting the feeling I have to invent every other word.

Maybe I could talk about him in a very past tense, in the past perfect, then there would be lofty poems in lofty Lausanne. We look at the past and see that nothing has been lost. Around the kidneys it has been completely preserved, further up is *el anima*, and everything is in perfect order to the tips of the toes, except you have to clear your throat, if only because there's an embarrassed cough stuck in it, and why shouldn't you when even Don Quixote often has to cough after a long silence.

One day his mouth will be described, we'll find out then what details they include, and his nose, the temperature of his breath and skin, the length of his legs, their circumference, and later the song will go one step further, in a remote past tense, for good measure.

Right now I can say with some certainty that the original is what people want, or rather, the non-translation is infinitely desirable. And I can talk about how quickly recognition happens. Loosely curled hair, slightly narrowed eyes, or at least eyes that aren't wide open, largely concealed, sly, secret eyes, it's really all about the gaze. What does recognizing someone even mean. I recognized him before I had seen his eyes, but I still couldn't make a phantom sketch of his facial composite.

At our last breakfast together Pierre asked quickly about the bookstore, and whether I still kept all the Insel Verlag books on the same shelf. He had once wanted to write a book someday, just one slim book like that, that would be enough. Right, well he had once wanted to be a sailor too.

We go up to the room again, it's eleven, the curtains have been half-drawn, the suitcases half-packed, and he paces slowly from the balcony to the bath, to the beds, to the table with two chairs. So this was the room I shared with you, he says as he paces up and down, and I happen to like the pace of his gait. People hardly talk about tempo, all we know is that swans start by aligning their pace and movements with each other, and I like his gait.

Then someone knocks at the door, Pierre looks straight at me, and two policemen come in. They show us their badges. They ask where we were the previous night. The guest in the room next door, a woman, has been found dead. About forty years old, she was found lying on her back, a fall could not be ruled out, but it also wasn't the only possibility. Did we hear anything? I ask Pierre. We ask the questions around here, the young policeman says in French, before repeating himself for my benefit in strange-sounding German. They ask us where we were. Someone in the green house across the street had seen Pierre climb across the wall that separated the two halves of the shared balcony.

What does it mean that someone saw him? We step out to the balcony and look at the glass wall, the policemen call us back at once. Whatever you say about the balcony, I know he was here all night, he was here.

Maybe someone was dreaming or confused Pierre with someone else, I say.

No, we aren't married, Pierre says. Well then is there something serious between you? The language barrier again, I think to myself, and Pierre is silent. He looks at me and asks the policemen how we can help, perhaps we could all take a look at the room next door, but the policemen exchange glances and decide to question us separately, and then they immediately separate us.

What will you be able to remember? Memory is like a tiny blanket that has to be pulled this way and that, sometimes the stomach is peeking out, sometimes it's the buttocks, sometimes you don't remember the stomach, sometimes the buttocks, but it turned out that I could describe every detail of what happened the previous night.

13

320 Characters

LA DONNA È MOBILE

The heat of summer had settled on the park, and he was able to pace about alone with his thoughts. Then, of all people, the woman he'd been thinking about for days appeared, umbrella in hand. He stood there, trying in his serious way to find one sentence that would convey everything to her, and ended up saying "Hello."

Somewhere a mobile phone is ringing, somewhere nearby, it has a pleasant ringtone. No one answers. It's a dove cooing in a convincingly even tone, which sounds as if someone is being called, persistently and implacably, or being pleaded with, someone is being pleaded with right this moment, that will do them some good.

A man three seats along notices us listening knee to knee, it's partly the music, but now he is embarrassed because no one was supposed to catch him glancing repeatedly at his watch, he hasn't heard a thing, he tells us that we'll hear nothing if we're sitting that way, which makes me temporarily unable to hear at all.

The lover unbuttons his shirt and has these other facial features, not really a smile, he takes his shoes off, throws himself onto the bed, lies on his back, and wants a shot of whisky to share, for us two, he looks exactly the way he used to years ago, the way he's always looked, I'm holding the glass, and these hours

are different from those hours at dinner in Locarno, where one evening in a villa something like forty dinner guests were expected, I no longer remember precisely how many. They came after a concert, well dressed and determined to stay in their concert mood, ate and drank until past midnight, and early the next morning

they realized that they could no longer leave the house, they only came to that realization gradually. Imagine how they must have looked at each other, admitting that they wouldn't be able to leave, neither one by one, nor all at once: they stayed in the villa for days despite wanting to escape, and that we don't want.

He got there after I did and waited in the hall by the tracks, where the shaft of light from one side always cut across the shaft from the other side, where he was standing there was only light, he didn't move and it was beautiful, I walked further along, and he looked at me as if he'd been waiting for me to look over.

People are filing out of the cinema as if they were coming from mass, streaming out of the exit at the back, moving slowly through the urban courtyard past urban houses like cattle moving through a feed passage. Hopefully the calves and cows and everyone in a narrow passage believes they are about to see something new.

In the subway, she sat next to a stranger and begged him to protect her from the man they could both see outside on the platform. She quickly told him all about her life, all about this pursuer and how he was pestering her. In the mind of the man on the subway, her words became a series of black-and-white photographs.

He brought her home and took the train back into the city, planning to rent a car and escape with her. On the way he saw an enlarged photo of her in the newspapers, and when he got home he held her in his arms as the pursuer entered and handed her over to him wordlessly. The beautiful, mad woman with her photo-stories.

Just after seven he came out of his own room, the single room he lived in, and walked along the corridor toward the communal bathroom. On the way, between one door and the next, a fat dove got in his way, and then the ground slipped out from beneath his feet, he could think of nothing but the ground he'd lost long ago.

The old people climbed the steep streets, panting, wheezing, shoving each other along, stumbling over each other. A camera team was filming the scene, observing them so carefully that they were able to capture not just the miserable paraphernalia in each of the old people's various bags, but also their dead-tired past.

Who said it happened in Zurich. It didn't, not even the train accident did. Zurich has never come to my mind in these stories, it probably hasn't come to Pierre's mind either, he hardly knows the city, he only spent one day in Zurich, that was years ago. Now and again he talks about Geneva, but only every now and then.

There's a cell phone ringing and this time it belongs to the second lead actress, who actually begins to sing, her song turns out to be about how no one could possibly mistake that unmistakable figure, her own, because no one else has a figure quite like hers, and then she presses the red button and waits contentedly.

And the stories, those favorite stories of ours that come to mind every now and again, do they just melt into thin air when we're not thinking about them? Not at all, he says, at night they lie in the park, under the bed, I bet they're there together, they still belong to us, and they're not discontent with their fate.

It used to be possible to roll the windows down in a train compartment, in Salzburg vendors with food carts would wait on the platforms passing steaming sausages, crispy rolls, and drinks into the carriages through the windows. Pierre boarded in Salzburg, and I've known him since then, we traveled to Milan via Zurich.

There's something missing here, and Pierre also falls silent. Oh it'll come to me, he says opaquely. What were we just talking about? No idea. A Russian book, yes but which one? This kind of forgetting is not a forgetting at all, it's a hole in the head, and eventually we'll find that we ourselves are falling right in.

On Wednesday she went to visit blind Mr. W. for the first time, the man she was meant to read to in the evenings. After only half an hour, he said she must have a child, maybe two, he could tell by her voice, then she kept reading from "The Lady with the Dog," and he told her that he could tell she was unusually happy.

She ran down the hill, in an old film, beside a tree on the hilltop she'd opened a telegram and read that her husband, the man who was everything to her, how else could you put it, was dead, and she ran down the hill as if she was almost flying; she'd had everything with him, she cried, they'd had everything wonderful.

Most of the words had already been locked out when a guest sat down at the table. The ones that had been locked out heard what the words that had been let in were saying in public, nasty things, hardly one sentence was true, the locked-out words were crying: Open the door! The door was not opened, and there were tears.

Joy: Select, Great Joy, Select, Enable, Delete, Go Back, Select Joy, Enable, and press the red button on the bottom left to go back to the main page. There is actually Joy, Great Joy without buttons, what'll they come up with next! Select, Backspace, Rename Joy: Happiness. Select. Send, Call, or Reply Via Text Message.

Not just drinking, eating too, leaning forward or sitting back, and the way we used to eat, sitting across from each other or next to each other, eating, pausing, dipping bread in the gravy, that's the part he always remembers, then we finish our memories off together, remembering again, pausing, and continuing to eat.

The waiter brought some boiled meat and cabbage in a bowl, then we were served red beets and even sour cream. Russian, I said. But we could barely look the waiter in the eye while he was telling us about the menu. His tongue was always visible, and it was the yellow tongue of an old, disappointed, really agreeable man.

Once we saw someone standing in the cherry tree and thought it was the waiter. The man shook the branches, the cherries thudded to the ground. I only knew of this way of handling cherries, of shaking them from trees, from a certain song. Then the man in the tree turned around, suddenly the waiter vanished, and we found a young man staring at us instead. Certain shapes of heads are common here, but you would search in vain for an oval-shaped face, for instance, or a heart-shaped one. Not that the shape itself means all that much, or I wouldn't be talking about heads and faces that I've known for a long time, that mean something to me.

At first she stood by the window with her back to him and wept. He had ordered a cup of tea for himself via room service. Again she had come to meet him in the city, again a little sadly, and they finally began to make plans not to have to meet in secret. The most difficult time was still ahead of them, they knew that.

Here people marvel at the fog. The seagulls are huge, almost tipping forward on their long legs. Where does the word seagull come from? Is it sad? Seagulls, wild ducks, cherry orchards, sour cherries. Spend a few days with them in the fog and the gulls will tell you about the word's origins, they might even sing of it.

There is a constant flickering inside you, perhaps because you've discovered a hidden weeping, a sobbing, a seagull screeching in a voice you know well, and that little sound makes you tumble through the throat of the person talking. Quick, write a song about it, save, rename the song later, do not delete, do not send.

The past is beginning shortly, it's starting soon, just a moment please, it has its plans, that's why it's about to start something, it hasn't happened yet, but soon it will tear through like the sunrise, except that *like* the sunrise isn't quite the right word. It will appear all of a sudden and be immediately visible.

Three men with the same silhouette, an old man, a very young man, and the one who's mine, but further off in the background a tiny midget is kicking and struggling, he can even be heard at night, and you shouldn't stare then. Don't stare! It's dangerous to look at someone that way! Something terrible is going to happen.

Seven people are talking all at once about happiness, chattering fiercely about unhappiness, it is becoming impossible to understand a word they say, they take turns outdoing one another in an irritable buzz that only gets softer or louder, but amidst the collective noise the word bliss, bliss, bliss keeps jutting out.

This emotion is taking shape, hot and metal-cold, to be sure, and it's just as moody or sensitive as ever, that's to say the emotion was sensitive, which means that the sensation was emotional, that doesn't sound good, but who knows, his gaze alone, Pierre's gaze! At any rate, it's clear that something is taking shape.

So-called swan parallels consist in the perfectly synchronized movement of the swans, the direction they're looking, their breathing in together, the sensation in their legs when walking, any sensation in the limbs, that's what it comes down to, what they are like when they wake up, when listening closely and so forth.

In London he sat on a bench in the fog. A young man approached him, and he knew the young man was himself, he was whistling a tune only the two of them knew, or only he knew. But the younger man didn't believe him. The older man actually saw the young man, but he was only dreaming of the older man, the man he'd become.

I recognized him right away, knew him at first glance, he was barely even visible but I saw him, and the first time I saw him, I also recognized him right away. It's like that with voices too, it is said that human beings can distinguish between hundreds of voices, even over the phone, even when the connection is bad.

Misunderstandings can poison opportunities like this. For instance, M. wouldn't have set foot in the port tavern of his own free will, he had nothing to do with the woman he'd just met, who made a commission for steering him in, and after he had been tricked into the tavern, he sang his great song of the ill-tempered.

He drank one glass of wine after another and sang his gloomy song of the fickleness of women, while his secret listener couldn't make heads or tails of the involved situation in his song. She had fallen into a trap, and she was stabbed to the ground before she could even figure out the trap. A fateful misunderstanding.

Experiments! In the worst-case scenario you'll just pay for it, there's time for trial and error before anything happens, and it's all voluntary so you can't complain! You could end up shivering in spring and glowing in winter for twenty-one years, all because of one glance. If you're still tempted, you can't complain.

Because of a particular look, now that I like. Because of a voice. Because of a lover and man oh man, just once for the lover or for his sake, when he has that look in his eyes, how can I put it, you could spend years trying to describe it. When he's got that look or tone of voice that promises to illuminate something.

A., for instance, is lying in a huge and hideous landscape, lying on his back and looking at the sky above him. Lying there he sees whatever happens to come into view right then, the sky with its various colors, and he gazes up at it until his questions simply disappear in the air. I, on the other hand, am certain that

no one is independent of his surroundings. If someone looks into the distance, he'll feel distant; if he looks at bright light, he'll feel bright; if he looks at fog, he'll feel foggy; if he looks at high, narrow mountains, he'll feel narrow; if he looks at high, distant mountains, he's going to feel high and distant.

She'd stopped crying, she turned away from the window, and they began to make plans. No more secret journeys, no more secret meetings. They had quite a difficult time ahead of them, he said. But they could talk to each other now, it grew dark as they kept making plans, and without noticing it they had shed their fears.

Three ravens sat in the tree in front of the house. They must be crows, he said, ravens don't come in flocks. But three birds don't make a flock, and when they fly off one by one and come back to perch on a branch, they seem lonely, particularly when they land on the ground instead. Maybe they're a new breed of ravens.

All these people look the same and wear precisely the same clothes. The sun shines, a gusty sun, and the sea doesn't care about these people one bit. They eat identical portions and their apartments are confusingly similar. But on Mondays the butchers come from the mainland bringing mincemeat, and the island is Utopia.

We're just coming out of the cinema as if we were coming from mass, although the film made us laugh: a man and a woman are parting glumly, he whispers extensively in her ear, and then they both look relieved, but the audience has to make up the words he whispered, they have to translate the man's words for themselves.

It isn't true that everyone falls in love every spring and even winter, and when they do butterflies appear; these are only interludes, and about once every hundred years, once a sae-culum, things are different, which may not be fair, that's why no one likes to talk about it, people would rather talk about spring fever.

I am living in the hotel where, years ago, a packet of cigarettes and a lighter (which I still have) lay waiting for me in my hotel room, with fruit on the table and a note with a few lines from my father. Pierre is also in the habit of putting a plate of fruit on the table wherever we are. Right now he isn't here yet.

Then, clutching the fruit, oh I don't know, we are in the Alps again, surrounded by the French that draws nearer in the Alps, I am happy, exhausted, Pierre asks me a question while I'm not listening, and then he says, I should permit him not to tell me everything. His light-gray eyes grow opaque, he goes to the window,

he is standing there, I look at him, and I too permit myself not to tell him everything, I don't even tell myself everything, and again I see a flickering in him. Or in me. Like the digital time display on my cell phone, a line of numbers that moves around the screen, appearing at the top, the bottom, or in the center.

In Geneva we saw the film about the butcher's daughter who passed herself off as a surgeon. We need not have done that to ourselves. A heavy-handed horror story, even though slashing and chopping happens plenty in real life, and not just in slaughterhouses. But who wants to talk frankly about that anyway, Pierre says.

In the dining car five people of different ages sit together, all exceedingly contented, they like everything, being old, being young. They eat the terrible microwaved meals good-naturedly, as if they really relish every bite. They're probably doing absolutely everything there is to enjoy, but only out of sheer effort.

The second lead actress has been listening in, and now she is making her entrance. She announces that she wants to be naked, undressed, not dressed. We dim the lights to make her comfortable. Everyone wants to be naked, I say, every *woman* does, she replies. Any other wishes? I ask. Everyone gets three wishes, you know.

Right then something crashes to the ground. It has been a sublime afternoon, and in the evening the stretch of land along the black lake is barely visible, even though the waterfront is lit as far as the eye can see. A man is walking unnoticed along the tracks, and he leaps onto the rails at precisely the right moment.

The train arrives on time and leaves on time from platform eight. It speeds along the tracks, crosses an icy bridge over the River Aare, crosses the rushing water in the river before sunrise on a cold morning, there's another bridge, and then it stops suddenly, everyone lurches forward, there's someone under the train.

A train is emerging from the tunnel, or better yet, bursting

out of the tunnel. It arrives on time in Olten. Later, somewhere in the southern region of the Alps, that same train
disappears again into yet another tunnel, and at the next
bridge for many moments the thunder of carriages rushing
over the edge can be heard.

First he goes over the rails, then Karenina, then I, or rather
first Anna, and then Pierre, but there's nothing at all left
for me, nothing I can do, it's finally over, and sure enough,
in the book which is essentially about bullfighting, it says
that all stories, if you only observe them for long enough,
end in death.

I am sitting in the corner on the end of the last row, watching, and later Pierre tiptoes over and sits down next to me
wordlessly, he's making some notes. Look, that's us, he whispers, and he isn't disappointed when I can't find us in the
movie, surely I've overlooked something. I'll tell you where
later, he whispers.

You're inside love with me like a dove, she says, she climbs
onto his lap, sitting on his knees, and kissing him on the
neck, on the shoulders and on the mouth, unflustered, as
though this were a necessary response, and yet she isn't
always sure she knows what she's doing, although it doesn't
feel like she is dreaming.

Tomorrow there'll be a party and all the words that were
locked up will be allowed out, many have long since known
that things will work out, I don't know why they haven't

discussed just how well it's all working out. No one wants to admit it, but once in a saeculum things can go well, and they're going well right now.

ZSUZSANNA GAHSE was born in 1946 in Budapest, from which she fled with her parents to Austria during the 1956 revolution. She grew up in Vienna and Kassel, and currently lives in Switzerland. She has published twenty-five books, and has translated the works of Hungarian writers such as Péter Esterházy and Péter Nádas into German. Recent works include *JAN, JANKA, SARA und ich* (Edition Korrespondenzen, 2015) and *More Than Eleven*, an opera libretto for mezzosoprano. She has received numerous prizes for her work, including the Aspekte-Literaturpreis (1983) and the Adelbert-von-Chamisso-Preis (2006). Since 2011 she has been a member of the Deutsche Akademie für Sprache und Dichtung.

CHENXIN JIANG was born in Singapore and grew up in Hong Kong. She has been awarded a PEN/Heim Translation Fund grant for Ji Xianlin's *The Cowshed* (New York Review Books, 2016), as well as the 2011 Susan Sontag Prize for Translation for her work on Goliarda Sapienza. Chenxin is the Senior Editor covering Chinese writing at *Asymptote*, an online journal of contemporary literature in translation. She studied comparative literature at Princeton University.